CASSIE MINT

Seeing Double

BLACK CHERRY
PUBLISHING

Contents

III   Fake Model

IV   Fake Maid

Keep in touch with Cassie!

Want to stay up to date with new releases, sales, and more instalove goodness?

Sign up for Cassie's newsletter!

1

Swapped Bride

Garrett

The decision is simple. Mountford wronged me—he tried to humiliate me and poach my suppliers; tried to swoop in on my territory. I know the man is a sniveling wretch, but this is an insult I cannot allow.

I could bankrupt him, of course. Take his mansion; his staff; his businesses. His offshore accounts and gaudy fleet of sports cars. If anything, I'd be doing the man a favor—for an art dealer, he has terrible taste.

But no. Those are just possessions, *things.* He'd make more money to replace what I took; he'd lean on his shady partners to help him back up to the top.

If I ruin him that way, it will be temporary. Unsatisfying. A sugar hit followed by an inevitable slump.

And I want to *ruin* him. I want him gutted and hollow; I want him to lay awake in his bed at night, sweating and trembling at the horror of what I've done. I want him to know, down to his wretched bones, that he brought it on himself.

That he roused me. He poked the beast. Angered the *Fox.*

And he paid the price.

Even now, the memory of his insolence makes my teeth clench. My pulse hammers in my throat, violence raging in my chest. To an outside observer, I would appear completely calm—bored, even.

Inside, I'm a maelstrom. And I will have my vengeance.

So if not his ugly sports cars, then what? It's simple, really. There is only one thing in this whole universe which Mountford prizes above all else.

His daughter, Lily. The prize of the city. A famed beauty, and the muse of fashion photographers everywhere. Oh, Mountford trots her out like a pedigree poodle, grinning for the cameras. His smug face says it all: *"You like her, huh? She's mine, mine, mine."*

As if her famed beauty is from *him*, with his sunken eyes and thinning silver hair. Pathetic old fool. Well, there's nothing else for it. I lean back in my desk chair, drumming my fingers on the mahogany wood, then gust out a sigh and pound her name out on my keyboard. A few clicks, and there she is: Lily Mountford.

Soon to become collateral damage.

I enlarge her photo, scrolling through the street fashion shots. She's a natural in front of the camera—all creamy skin and soft, caramel waves. I twist my mouth, considering her, but...

Nothing. I feel nothing.

I get more aroused looking at the black market paintings in my private gallery.

No matter. I'm not going to hurt her, after all. She will be my wife only in name. A possession to dangle over her father's head, lest he get ideas above his station again. I scroll through

Lily's information, already bored, and my eyes snag on one detail.

Siblings: Twin sister, deceased.

Mountford had twins? I've never heard of another daughter. She must have died long ago. Before he started bothering me, jostling for dominance in the art dealing world.

I look at Lily's photos again, looking for signs of grief. Perhaps we will have something in common after all. A shared darkness that we might bond over. She may not move me physically, may not interest me sexually, but if she is to be my wife, it would be preferable to get along.

Preferable, but not essential. If she's as tiresome as her father—and she surely must be, given the way he dotes on her—I'll pack her off to Europe to one of my empty homes. She can spend her days posing in vineyards, or volunteering for homeless shelters, or whatever it is bored wives do.

I don't need to want her. Hell, I don't even need to *like* her.

Like I said. Collateral damage.

I lean closer to the screen, staring at her face in photo after photo. But there are no shadows clinging below those emerald eyes; no strain around her mouth. By all accounts, she is happy. Perfectly content with life, never mind her dead twin.

What a brat. If I'd had someone to call family, someone to band together with while growing up, nothing would shatter my loyalty. I'd be ruined to find myself without them. Instead, I'd been alone, left to fend for myself, forced into darkness—

I shut the thought down. I know from experience: it leads nowhere useful.

"My apologies, Lily," I murmur to myself, the words sounding empty to my own ears. I'm *not* sorry. This must be done. Her father must learn the consequences of his actions. I snatch my phone off the desk, dial without looking, and press it to my ear.

My assistant answers on the first ring, his voice calm.

"Yes, Mr. Taylor?"

"Reach out to Mountford. Relay this message word-for-word." I smirk at my monitor, eyes still trained on Lily. It's a pity, really, that her appearance leaves me cold. "I've chosen my price for his indiscretions. He can agree, or I'll take every last cent he owns."

"Very good, sir. What is the price?"

"His daughter, Lily." I scrub a hand over my jaw. "She will be my bride."

Nora

I bound off the sofa in my private suite, arms pinwheeling as I remember the wet nail polish on my toes a moment too late. My feet scrunch into the rug, my arms flailing as I catch my balance, then I huff and bend down to inspect the damage.

"Phew!" I straighten up, flipping my golden brown hair out of my face with a smile. "They can still be saved."

No one replies. I do this a lot—talk to myself in the silence. Apart from Lily, no one ever comes up to my floor, tucked away as it is in the tower.

You'd think my father built his mansion like this on purpose, just to lock his daughter away in a turret.

Not Lily, though. Lily can go where she likes. She's his pride and joy. And I was too, back when we were little, our perfect faces bright and unmarred.

It all changed after the accident. The ice skating lesson which ended with a deep gash scored through my cheek. I was lucky to be alive, the doctors said in the hospital—a few inches lower and the skate could have slit my throat.

My father didn't see it that way. All he saw was my scar, and what it meant: spoiled goods.

"You'll never make a name for yourself now," he'd growled as he took me home from the hospital. "What use are you to me?"

I was eight years old.

Eleven years later, and those words still sting. They echo in my mind whenever I glance in the mirror and catch a glimpse of that angry scar. Brushing my teeth is a minefield; getting dressed is an exercise in avoiding my own gaze.

At least I don't have to worry about looking presentable. Not like Lily—she agonizes over her outfits, terrified that the press will rip her to shreds.

"This is my way out," she told me once. "If I can do this, if I can become a model or an actress, I'll be *free.* And I'll take you with me," she'd added quickly, squeezing my arm. "We'll be together."

We linked pinkies, and I nodded.

"Together. Always."

So that's one benefit of being locked away, all because of a stupid scar. No one scrutinizes my appearance, and thank God! My skin goes all hot and flushed just thinking about it. I'm left here in peace, and though it may be boring, I get to work on my designs.

Nail art. New color combinations. Ways of creating patterns and using tiny jewels. I get better with every design I try, and the followers of my secret social media accounts think so too.

Rapunzel Designs, I've called my little venture. Lily has her looks—well, this is *my* way out.

My father can't keep me locked up here forever. He just can't.

8

"Lil?" I call out now, my painted toes saved. I could have sworn I heard the door open.

Slow footsteps come down the hall, creaking over the floor-boards, then my sister stands in the doorway. I squeal, excited to see her, shuffling forward with my arms outstretched, but something makes me stop.

She looks... not just sad. She looks *ruined*.

Lily is deathly pale, her beautiful features drawn. Her usually plump, rosy lips are bloodless. She darts out her tongue to wet her lip, then clears her throat to speak.

Silence rings through the tower.

My twin sister bursts into tears.

"Lil?" I ask, alarmed, forgetting my toes and running forward. She falls into my arms, sobbing into my shoulder. I can barely catch what she's saying, she's howling so much, but I hear a few words.

Father.

Sold.

Marriage.

No, that can't be right. Our father *loves* Lily. After all, she's the beautiful one. She's the one who brings him attention and prestige, who he can dangle in front of potential business partners to distract them and strike good deals.

If he *sold* her somehow, he'd lose all of that. I shake my head hard, my ears ringing.

"Lil. Stop. Tell me again, slowly."

She hiccups loudly, burying her face in my neck. Then she straightens up, her eyes hard but her lip wobbling, and scrubs her sleeve over her wet, shining face.

"He's given me away," she says, voice hoarse. "Sold me like one of his paintings. He's making me marry the Fox, Nora."

9

I shudder. Everyone's heard of the Fox. The man is a legend in the art world, famed for pulling off impossible heists and striking billion dollar deals.

He's cold. Brutal. Even worse than our father. I shake my head hard, gathering Lily back into my arms.

"No. No, he can't have you. They can't *sell* you, Lily, you're a human being!"

"You know it's not that simple," she whispers, and my heart sinks like a stone.

I *do* know. Our father is not a good man. He does business in the shadows; there is blood on his hands. If he wants something from his people, we make it happen, or heads roll. Literally.

Perhaps not us. But if not us, someone we care for. And for Lily…

I'm her weakness. I'm the reason she's going through with this.

My heart breaks into a thousand pieces in my chest. The only person I love, the only person who loves *me*—gone. Sold to a monster.

I'll never see her again. And who knows what horrors await her with the Fox?

I guide Lily over to the sofa, still sobbing in my arms, and sit her down on the cushions. Her voice cracks as she cries, and every whimper feels like a punch to my stomach.

"If I m-marry him, I'll never… I'll never be with…" Lily bursts into tears again, burying her face in a cushion. I smooth a palm over her trembling back, up and down between her shoulder blades, my brain whirring a mile a minute.

Lily may be resigned to her fate, but *I'm* not. And the beginnings of a plan swirl in my mind.

Lily does not want to marry the Fox.

And I do not want to stay here.

Oh sure, an arranged marriage is not how I'd *choose* to leave, but perhaps it's a blessing. An opportunity.

I'll play the role. Trick the Fox. And be swept out of this house with him once and for all. Then, the second his guard is down, I'll sneak away. I'll finally start my own life, not locked away in this tower.

It's reckless. It's *crazy.* There are a thousand things that could go wrong. But my heart swells in excitement.

"Lily." I nudge my crying twin. "Dry your eyes. I've got a plan."

Garrett

I never planned to take a wife. Women have been little more than distractions to me—always scheming and wanting something. My riches, my artworks, my prestige. A ticket to fortune and fame.

I don't blame them. Hell, I respect them for it. But I'm no one's mark.

It is tiresome, then, to find myself in a wedding tux. The fabric is dark and soft, perfectly tailored, with a crisp, snowy white shirt underneath. As I linger in a hallway, some brave or foolish soul tucks a flower into my button hole.

I let it happen. Beautiful things are my kryptonite.

Speaking of beautiful things—there is no sign of my future wife. There have been no communications beyond Mountford's grudging acceptance. He was blustery and casual about it, trying to pass it off in the gentleman's club as a mutual idea.

As if anyone would want *me* as a son in law. I'm twice his daughter's age, and lethal behind my bored smile. I've ended lives, stolen wonders. Toppled kingpins.

So, fine. Mountford can laugh and pretend that this was all his doing. That he's tamed the beast, not fallen prey to its ire.

We both know the truth. Everyone else does, too. The man can't even sustain his own lie. For example: this wedding that is supposedly his idea, this joining between his precious daughter and his new 'ally'—there is no reception planned. No well wishers invited. No gleeful paparazzi.

Only one each of our employees to act as witnesses, Mountford himself, and the bride.

Please. He's no worthy opponent.

If the roles had been reversed, I'd have covered my humiliation with a grand party, the likes of which the city had never seen. I'd have buried any doubts under a landslide of opulence, celebrating the 'happy' occasion.

Instead, Mountford is sulking. Short-sighted child.

No matter. I would have skipped the reception anyway.

"Well?" I snap as my assistant James approaches. A young man in his early twenties, James was an unlikely choice, but I favor competence over empty experience. James is sharp and efficient, seemingly tireless in his commitment, and has no family life to distract him from his work.

"She's coming." James comes to a halt at my side, his eyes darting over my appearance. He may be committed to his work, but he won't candy his words. If I look a fool, he will tell me so.

Yes, he's a valuable asset.

"The button hole's a nice touch," James murmurs as we watch the priest duck through a nearby doorway. Out in the main chapel, string music quavers to life. It's unearthly and aching, the sound bouncing off the stone walls, and I swallow hard.

Now is no time for sentiment.

"Will she go through with it?" I grit out. This is one fear that has kept me awake at night. It's no show of power if the pretty young thing publicly rejects me. Yes, her father would pay the price, but have I set myself up for a bruised ego?

A head pokes through the doorway, interrupting my clamoring thoughts. It's a middle-aged woman with neat blonde hair tied back in a bun and pursed red lips. Mountford's employee.

She clears her throat, boldly meeting my eye. I like her. Perhaps I'll offer her a better position with one of my companies.

"Whenever you're ready, Mr. Taylor. We'll begin."

I nod, my expression calm, even as my throat runs oddly dry. I stride forward, my footsteps echoing off the flagstones, James hurrying behind. As I duck through the chapel doorway, I almost stumble.

She's here. She's already at the altar.

Of course she is, I chide myself. There are no pews of onlookers to walk between—no loved ones to show off her dress for.

And what a dress.

Even at the far end of the aisle, its craftsmanship is clear. Perhaps Lily did not get the wedding of her dreams, but Mountford could not resist spoiling her one last time.

I'm glad he did. Ivory silk tumbles down her slender body, pooling on the stone floor. The back is cut low, flaunting her pale, delicate skin, the nub of her shoulder blades shifting as she fiddles with her bouquet. If I thought my mouth was dry in the hall, it's nothing compared to now.

Those shiny caramel curls, pinned up in intricate braids. That soft, floating veil edged with pearls.

There is a goddess waiting beside the altar. I want to fall to my knees and beg her forgiveness right here. I want to gather the slippery fabric of her gown and kiss the hem; I want to run my palms up those legs, over those rounded hips.

My feet carry me up the aisle on autopilot. As I near her, I catch a whiff of her scent. She smells like sugar and vanilla, a human cupcake, and my heart seizes in my chest when I remember.

There is no cake. I did not order a cake. I assumed we'd want to be out of each other's company as soon as possible. Before seeing her, I'd thought of our *wedding* with a sour taste in my mouth.

Now this angel is about to wed and has no cake to cut. No friends in the pews to admire her dress. No bridesmaids to catch her bouquet.

My blackened heart rends in two.

"Excuse me," I grind out and wheel away at the altar, marching to the side of the chapel to make a call. I bark instructions into the phone, my eyes fixed on the woman waiting for me. Her chin dips forward, her shoulders slumping.

I'm already disappointing her. God, I want to die.

My hands tremble as I race back to the altar, wiping my palms on my jacket. Her head twitches toward me, her face hidden by the veil, and the priest begins in a halting monotone.

I don't hear a word of it. Honor, accept, cherish, yada yada yada—this woman is *mine.*

Of course I'll cherish her. Honor her. Treat her like a treasure. I'm not a goddamn monster.

Okay, maybe I have been monstrous a time or two in my life—but no more.

She deserves better. She deserves everything.

My bride.

Nora

Jeez, he won't stop *staring*. He's not even listening to the priest!

Can he tell I'm not Lily? We used special extra-thick foundation on my cheek, and I have my veil, but the Fox's eyes are fixed on me, brooding and intense. A slight frown creases his forehead, like I'm a puzzle he can't figure out.

I'm annoying him already. Oh, God help me. Let me carry off this facade just long enough to escape his clutches.

Although...

He is awfully handsome. Older than me, yes, but not gone to seed like my father. The Fox—Mr. Taylor—has dark brown hair, only threaded with hints of silver at his temples. He's tall and broad shouldered, such a commanding presence that I have to tilt my chin up to look at him.

Pale gray eyes stare back at me, burning into my soul.

I shiver, my skin flushing hot all over beneath my gown, and my breasts grow heavy and tight.

Inside a house of God? Yeah, I'm definitely going to Hell.

It doesn't matter how good he looks, I tell myself sternly. He's

16

the reason I've been bought and sold in Lily's place. This man is a brute, who wants to steal my only sister away from me. Well, the joke's on him.

I don't feel so cocky when we say our parts out loud. My eyes flick to my father as I recite my lines: *"I, Lily Mountford..."*

My father huffs beside me, his leather shoes squeaking against the tile, but then it's over and he hasn't said a word. Hasn't loudly declared that I'm not Lily at all, that I'm a pretender who no one wants.

And he hasn't tried to undo this awful thing, tried to save his favorite daughter from this fate.

I turn my face and stare dry-eyed at the altar. My throat is tight, but something hardens in my chest, and I suck in a deep breath.

This man is no true father.

I refuse to look at him again, even when the Fox lifts my veil carefully over my head and bares my face for the first time. My father grunts in surprise, but we both ignore him. Me, I'm done with him, and the Fox is too busy running his greedy gaze over my features.

He darts out his tongue to wet his bottom lip. His mouth is strong and curved, his chin square with a cleft. I sway toward him in a trance.

"You may now kiss the bride." The priest raises his hands in celebration, though there are no crowds here to whoop and clap. I half expected we'd skip this part—that the Fox would snub my father one last time by refusing to kiss his prize.

How badly I've misjudged him. The words are barely out of the priest's mouth when the Fox gathers me into his arms. He crushes me against his chest, surrounding me completely, so big and broad and strong. He could snap me like a twig, and

17

yet he lowers his face to mine and kisses me so gently that my chest aches.

It's soft. Careful. It sends heat rushing through my body, pooling low between my legs. I sigh into his mouth, the priest and my father forgotten, and bow against him, pressing closer.

The Fox growls, his mouth hungrier now, taking my head in his hands and slanting our mouths to slide in his tongue. I gasp, head swimming, my skin buzzing with want, but the priest clears his throat.

I untangle myself and step back, heart pounding.

That's what I've been missing all these years in my tower? *That's* what kissing feels like? I want to run and whoop back down the aisle; I want to burst into the paved courtyard and shout to the heavens.

But of course, everyone else already knows about kissing. I'm the locked up fool.

The Fox—Mr. Taylor watches me again, his chest heaving under his shirt. Is he affected by me too? Oh, I hope so. I squeeze my thighs together, and his eyes darken.

"Let's go," he grits out, ignoring everyone else in the chapel and offering me his arm. I start to glance back at my father, but I stop myself. He'll discover our ruse soon enough, if he hasn't already.

He doesn't deserve my goodbyes. So I nod and smile at the priest, and trip forward to take my husband's arm.

Not a true husband, a voice hisses in my head as he leads me through the chapel corridors. He toys with my fingers as we walk in silence, shortening his strides so that I don't trip in my heels.

No. Our 'marriage' is a sham. He's married to Lily, or so he thinks. And since one sister's name is on the certificate while another said the words…

It's all a lie. Every part of it. Even that kiss was meant for Lily. And when I'm find out, he'll be furious—he'll hate me even more than my father.

I let him lead me in silence, my mood plummeting as we walk, until my lips turn down and my eyes brim with tears.

Oh, what have I gotten myself into?

And why does my heart feel like it's bleeding?

Garrett

Lily Mountford is nothing like her public persona. The press adores her, but she's always come across as flighty. Temperamental and a little wild.

This angel is the opposite. She bore the indignities of our sham wedding with a raised chin and straight back. She's an ocean of calm compared to my maelstrom. Even walking beside her, I feel my pulse settle.

Something tickles at my brain, a sneaking suspicion, but I quash it. The least I can do is give her my full attention.

Our car is ready and waiting at the back of the chapel, across a stone courtyard. For the thousandth time since laying eyes on her, I want to flog myself for not bothering with a proper wedding.

She is not the sort of woman you sneak out the back exit. She's someone to parade down the front steps, where everyone can see and admire her. Where she can draw the praise she deserves, damn it.

I'll fix this. I'll make it better.

"This way," I mutter, voice gruff from my tight throat. I tug her gently through a doorway, into a courtyard that smells like flowers and damp stone. Buttery sunlight spills between the chapel roofs, and it glints golden in her hair.

I'm so hard I could bite through my own tongue.

Instead, I usher her to the passenger side door. I *had* planned on depositing her in the back seat where we could try our best to ignore each other.

Everything has changed. I want her in the front with me, where I can touch her, look at her, listen to her husky voice.

"Thank you," she murmurs, reaching for the door handle. I snatch her hand and press her cool fingers to my lips. She watches me, a blush creeping over her cheeks, her mouth parting slightly.

I can't wait a second longer.

I crowd her back against the car, sealing our bodies together, moaning as our lips meet again. She kisses me back just as desperately, her hands scrabbling at my shoulders as she tries to get closer, tries to climb me like a monkey.

Her wish is my command. I scoop her up by the ass, a hand clenched on each of her juicy thighs. This time, when I press her against the car, my cock lines up with her core and we both suck in deep breaths.

"Beautiful girl." I drop my forehead against hers, rocking my hard length against her. I can't help it—God knows she deserves better, but the heat of her pussy is burning through her thin gown.

She wants me as badly as I want her. And by the dazed look on her face, it's her first time experiencing these things. That realization fills me with savage pleasure, and I rut harder against her, scraping my teeth down her throat.

"Mr…Taylor…" she grits out, her heels digging into the backs of my thighs, urging me on.

"Lily," I reply, and just like that, she wilts in my arms. Where she'd been clutching to me, writhing against my chest, she drops back against the car, arms loose. "No," I growl, slinging her arm back around my neck. I nip at her chin, my gut sinking. "No, don't turn me away."

"I'm not," she whispers, even as she slips out of my hold. Her heels scrape against the courtyard flagstones, and my blood roars in my ears. Somehow, I force my limbs into action, opening the door for her and guiding her inside. She murmurs in protest, but I buckle her in, double-checking the seat belt.

I pause, ducked inside the car, and suck in a lungful of her scent.

Sugar.

Vanilla.

And the faint tinge of arousal.

My eyes slam closed, and I straighten back up before I do something I regret. The cool air hits my cheeks, and I shake my head hard before shutting the car door.

Get it together.

You swore to be a husband, not a slathering beast.

It's hard, though, and gradually becomes an impossible task as my car eats up the miles. We roar down endless streets and highways, heading out of the city until the buildings drop away and the mountains rise up on all sides. The sky dims, the first stars winking, and the horizon burns orange as the sun sets.

She watches everything with her nose practically fixed to the glass, her breath fogging her window. Every tiny detail seems to absorb her in equal measure, from the office parks on the outskirts of the city to the soaring mountains and the ocean in the distance.

"Have you come out here before?" I ask, breaking the silence.

She chokes out a laugh, then cuts herself off.

"No," she says eventually. Her voice is so quiet, I have to strain to hear it over the engine. "No, never."

I hum, turning back to the road as it winds up into the mountains. I'm surprised—Lily Mountford is a famed beauty and budding model, after all. She must have been on plenty of shoots out in the picturesque wilds. The fashion magazines lining store shelves often show off her perfect face.

Funny. Her picture never moved me before, but the woman beside me in the car…

I'm ruined.

"I'm taking you home," I tell her, and it almost sounds like a threat. But she's *mine* now, and my home, my artworks, my empire—it's all for her.

I want to see her reaction when she steps into her new home for the first time.

Lily shrugs, turning to stare out of the window again. I swallow down a shard of glass in my throat.

Soon. I'll make her love me back soon.

It's all I live for now.

Nora

"Wait here."

The Fox is terribly severe. His face is as unyielding as the mountains around us, his strong cheekbones carved in stone. When he pulls up a long gravel driveway, the path lit on either side by old-fashioned lanterns, he throws the car into park and barks at me to stay put.

I squeak out a reply, mouth dry, but he's already gone. He throws himself out of the car, his broad shoulders disappearing into the dark evening sky, and slams the door shut.

I flinch. My fingers scrabble at my seat belt, but I've only just unclipped it when my car door wrenches open.

"Lily."

His voice is deep. Gruff. And when he says my sister's name like that, I want to rip his tongue out.

"Coming," I breathe, swinging my legs out of the car, tugging the skirt of my gown with them. It's breezy up here in the mountains, and cool night air washes around my legs. It catches in the light fabric, molding it to my calves and thighs, and the Fox grunts before he drops to his knees in the gravel.

"What are you—" I begin to ask, but he places a hand on each of my knees. He glances up from beneath lowered brows, his pale eyes burning straight through to my core. The breeze tugs at his hair, so dark it's almost black in the low light, and the glow from the nearby lantern pools golden over his skin. His tux jacket is abandoned somewhere in the car, and his shirt sleeves are rolled; his top buttons undone.

I suck in a shaky breath, my legs already trembling. My nipples pebble against my gown, and I lie to myself that it's because of the cold air.

"Are we going inside?" I whisper. For some reason, I can't find my voice.

The Fox nods. "In a moment." His thumbs skate over my knees through the fabric. Back and forth. Back and forth. My breath builds in my chest until I'm full to bursting, scratching at the car seats with my fingernails. My chest heaves, my skin burning hot under his perusal, until I can't take it anymore.

"Please."

His mouth twists, a savage kind of satisfaction playing over his face. Then he's pushing my knees apart, slow but firm, until the mountain breeze drifts up my skirt and plays over my private parts.

I whimper, tipping my head back. I wriggle on the seat, looking for—looking for *something*—

"Easy, baby girl." A soothing palm slides up my thigh, scorching a trail in its wake. I calm, resting my temple against the car door frame. I watch him with heavy-lidded eyes.

"Has anyone touched you here before?" he asks conversationally, trailing a blunt fingertip up the inside of my thigh. Goosebumps ripple over my skin, and I shake my head hard.

"Say it." He grips my thigh hard. It's rough and possessive, but it doesn't hurt—no. It sends a bolt of molten heat through my core.

"No," I gasp, swaying forward. His grip loosens again, the swoop of his thumb soothing. "No one has touched me there. Not... not even..."

He frowns at me, puzzled, then his eyebrows drift up his forehead. He drops back onto his heels, his gaze fixed on my panties as he slides my skirt higher.

"Not even you?" he asks quietly. I make sure to answer him this time.

"No." I hiccup. "Not even me."

The Fox likes that. Vicious satisfaction spreads over his face and he kneads my thighs harder. He's touching both legs now, creeping higher and higher to where the breeze plays over my soaked panties.

"I'm going to touch you everywhere. Every inch of you. I'll show you how it all feels, angel."

A flimsy strip of lace halts him. He glances at me, then smirks.

The Fox ducks his head beneath my gown before I can react, a shocked cry bursting out of my mouth. I grasp his shoulder, bunching his white shirt in my fist, but he sits back as quickly as he bent down.

Something dangles from his mouth. It's a strip of white lace, clenched between his teeth.

My garter.

"Oh," I murmur. I'm still clinging to his shoulder, tugging at him now. A kitten might as well push a panther. He grins at me again, dark and feral, and leans forward to nip at my lip. My garter flutters to the ground between us, lost to the evening darkness.

"Lily," he says, rubbing his nose over my cheeks. "I'm going to make you howl, sweet girl."

"Don't call me that," I gasp, my thoughts too muddled to remember my own lie. When he frowns at me, I splutter out an excuse. "I don't want to be called Lily anymore. I like sweet girl. I like angel."

He growls and lunges forward. His kiss is biting, punishing, but I take every thrust of his tongue and nip of his teeth with eager groans. He leans forward until my pebbled nipples brush against his chest, and I tug at his shoulders.

I want him closer.

Closer.

This wasn't the plan, I think distantly, but whatever this is between us… it's too powerful to deny. One look from this man makes my stomach swoop. A whiff of his masculine scent makes my panties damp.

Maybe the plan isn't doomed. I could still sneak away, and simply let the Fox enjoy me before then…

Even the thought of walking away from this man makes my chest cave in. When his arms are around me, when his gaze is on me, everything is *right*. Righter than it's ever been.

"I can't wait," he mutters, reaching beneath my gown and tearing my ivory lace panties clean off. The delicate fabric rips, fluttering to the gravel, then my legs are pushed wide again. I scrabble for the car roof, holding on for dear life as the Fox leans down and licks a broad stripe up my pussy.

"Oh!" I bite my lip, the lights of the city below us blurring. He licks me again and my hips twitch up.

"Needy little thing, aren't you?" He bands an arm across my hips, holding me down. And oh, that feeling of being pinned, of being restrained by this man—I moan and rock against him.

His tongue is wet and warm, delving through my folds, exploring every inch of me. He finds a tight bundle of nerves and bears down on it, licking and sucking, and I can't help it—I cry out, long and loud.

"*Yes*," he growls, shifting to slide the tip of one finger inside me. He rubs at my entrance, circling, then dips just inside before retreating. I moan, bucking up harder. "Call out for me, angel. Let the whole city know who owns you now."

"You do!" I sob, tremors wracking my thighs.

Below us, twenty feet from the driveway, car headlights pass along the mountain road. The driveway is lit—someone need only glance up here and they'd see it all. The Fox on his knees, his broad shoulders stretching his white shirt, his head buried between my thighs. I stare at those passing headlights, each groan dredged deeper from my body, and when the Fox returns to that bundle of nerves and suckles on it, I explode. My chin tucks to my chest, my muscles locking and spasming, and I can't hear anything except the rush of blood in my ears.

Gradually, I float back to earth. My feet drop to the gravel beside his hips, and I look up at the Fox with wide eyes.

"What…" I'm still dizzy. I shake my throat and try again. "What *was* that?"

He chuckles, smoky and dark.

"That was you coming on my tongue." He chucks me under the chin and stands up. "You'd better get used to it."

Garrett

For the first time in decades, I'm nervous. My new bride trips along the driveway beside me, her heels catching in the gravel. I steady her elbow, making a mental note to have the entire driveway repaved.

Her breath still saws in and out of her lungs as the flush of intimacy fades from her cheeks. Her nipples prod through her thin gown like two points, and I grit my jaw so hard I'm surprised my teeth don't crack.

Restraint.

I need to give her space. Not *rush* her.

I already pushed my luck when I buried my face in her delicious pussy.

The front door swings open ahead of us, the doorman murmuring his welcome as we pass into the lobby. My wife stares around with wide eyes, her fingers plucking nervously at the beading on her gown.

I clear my throat. "Leave us." The doorman vanishes without a word, melting into the background. In the distance, there are the faint sounds of food preparation, and Lily flinches at the crash of a pan.

I scrub a hand over my face. It would be… wrong, to stride into the kitchens and put the fear of God into my staff.

Not right now, anyway. Maybe later, when my wife no longer vibrates with tension. She stands ramrod straight in the center of the lobby, gazing in turn at the oil paintings decorating the walls. There are famous impressionist paintings; wild landscapes; intimate portraits which bring that blush back to her cheeks.

"Do you like art?" I ask quietly, then hold my breath until she answers. For once, she spins toward me, a bright smile stretching her cheeks.

"Oh, I *love* art. Especially—"

She breaks off, her eyes dropping to the marble floor. I want to grab her shoulders and shake them; I want to roar and pound on my chest until she *finishes that damn sentence.*

"Especially what?" I croak. She blushes impossibly redder, and when she answers it's in a whisper.

"Nail art," she tells me, face miserable. I snatch up her hand, flipping it over to inspect her fingernails. Nothing. Only a pearly white sheen. Yanking up a fistful of her gown, I check her toes next in her strappy heels, but they're matching white. She stumbles back, almost tripping over her own feet, and I gather her against my chest. I tuck her there, her head under my chin, as I tilt her fingers in the light from the chandelier.

"It's stupid," she mumbles.

"It's not stupid," I bark. "You will show me."

"I don't—I don't have my things."

Of course not. I stole her away here with nothing but the gown on her back, too goddamn greedy to get my hands on her to think straight.

"You will. Order replacements, new supplies—whatever you want. But you will show me, do you understand?"

She nods, sniffling against my chest. Can she hear my pounding heartbeat? Surely, she must be able to. Hell, the *neighbors* must be wondering what that racket is. My shocked, ill-used organ is flinging itself against my rib cage, battling to get to *her*.

I'm fucking this up. Being so gruff with her; burying my tongue between her legs before she's ready. My sweet angel is trembling like a leaf in my arms, and it takes the last ounce of my willpower to drop my arms and step away. She blinks up at me, still half dazed, a glassy sheen to her emerald eyes.

I made her cry. God fucking damn it. I want to get down on my knees and slam my head against the marble.

Instead, I gesture across the lobby. She follows my hand, trepidation creasing her brow. The mansion is not welcoming at first sight, cut into the mountain and built from local rock. The decor is bold, all dark woods and statement art pieces—sultry oil paintings and abstract, twisting sculptures. Then there are the silent staff members, the distant sounds from the kitchen, and the dark sky spilling through the huge glass windows.

It must be a lot to take in.

"Nothing to be afraid of here, sweet thing." Nothing except me, and I would rather tear out my own throat than harm a single hair on her head. "Now why don't you explore your new home?"

Nora

I'm all jumbled up inside. Everything I expected the Fox to be—cold, merciless, cruel—he's the opposite. The way he treats me, you'd think we were true newlyweds and I was the love of his life. It's heady and jarring, and it makes heat pulse between my legs. I'm aching for him again, so awfully soon, and what will he think of me for that?

I try not to let on. I keep my eyes averted as he leads me through the rooms of his mansion. His home is nothing like I'd expected, either. I'd pictured minimal white box rooms and sparse furniture. Hard lines and stark shades.

Instead, his home is comfortable. Cozy, in an opulent sort of way. The rooms are filled with splashes of deep reds and blues, and the furniture is sculpted from polished wood. All except the sofas—they look sinfully comfortable, the perfect place to lie back and—

No. I cut myself off.

I can't get attached. Not more than I already have. He thinks I'm *Lily*, it's my sister he truly wants, and I need to make my escape before he finds out he's been tricked.

My sore heart throbs in my chest.

I don't want to go.

For a little while, I let myself play. I imagine that the hunger in his eyes is really for me; that these rooms truly will be my home now. The heavy curtains are soft as I trace my fingertips down the fabric, and my heels sink into a Turkish rug.

I kick my heels off, forgetting my manners, but the Fox growls in approval as I curl my toes in the rug.

"Yes. Get comfortable, angel. This is your kingdom, now."

My tower back home feels like a thousand miles away. Back there, I had three rooms: a tiny bedroom with a single bed, a cramped living space, and a bathroom. When I wanted to exercise, I had to find videos online that didn't involve any sideways movement.

The Fox leads me from room to room, gazing avidly at my face, watching my every reaction. And when my mouth falls open in shock at the master bathroom, a smirk tugs on his lips.

It's vast. Open to the mountains, with huge glass windows taking up the walls. An enormous stone bathtub takes up the center of the room, where the view stretches around on all sides.

"Would you like to bathe?" the Fox asks, his lips tickling my neck. I suck in a deep breath and nod.

A *bath*. I haven't had a bath since before my accident. Only cramped showers in a shadowed stall. Reality crashes into me, and I clap my hand to my cheek.

My scar.

My makeup.

I cannot bathe here.

I don't have any more makeup to hide who I really am. The

second I slide into that water, the game is up. So I back away from the bathtub, tugging on the Fox's sleeve.

"Wait, no. I changed my mind. Let's continue the tour."

He frowns at me, suspicion etched on his forehead, and my mouth runs dry. But he nods and strides out of the bathroom without argument, and I hurry to follow after. We trail around the rest of the mansion, and it's only when we reach the dining room, our wedding feast laid out and ready, that I realize he didn't show me any bedrooms.

My heart sinks. Does he not want me like that? Was I... strange, somehow, earlier in the car? Off-putting?

Or does he not trust me? He's been scowling since the bathroom, a muscle ticking in his jaw. I lower myself into the offered chair, my stomach growling at the delicious aromas even as my insides churn.

It's...

Wow. He spared no expense. In all truth, I hadn't expected a fancy dinner at all. We both know that he married me—well, 'Lily'—to spite my father. He needn't have bothered with *this*.

The table is covered with a crisp white table cloth and set with silver cutlery. Both of our napkins are folded into swans, and I poke at mine before I catch him staring.

There is a basket of warm rolls. A tureen of soup; a braised roast displayed in the center of the table. Vegetables provide bright pops of color, and a bottle of champagne sweats in an ice bucket.

The Fox glares at the food like it's some kind of insult. He sits back and huffs as a waiter in a cream jacket steps forward and pours us two glasses of champagne.

I start to speak, but no words come out. I clear my throat and try again.

34

"Don't you... don't you like it?"

He jerks his head toward me. I flinch away from the full force of his scowl, and his expression flickers.

He swallows. "No. It's not worthy of you."

I gaze around the food again, confused. It's the most incredible meal I've ever seen. Suddenly, I want so badly to tell him that. To explain that I've spent the last eleven years eating cold, congealed leftovers on a tray.

"It's perfect," I whisper instead. A large, white shape catches my eye over his shoulder, and I brighten. "There's cake, too!"

Just like that, his scowl crumbles. His eyes crease as he smiles at me, reaching over to drag my chair closer. I squeak, carried across the floorboards, but when our sides bump together something settles in my chest.

"Allow me." He plucks a warm bread roll from the basket, tearing off a small piece. I open my mouth automatically, gazing up at him with wide eyes, and his expression heats. The bread is fluffy and delicious on my tongue.

We eat like that for hours. The Fox barely bothers to eat at all, instead feeding me mouthfuls of every dish on the table. Occasionally, he calls out to the chef and insists another side is made. Another dessert prepared.

I sip from my champagne between mouthfuls, the zingy bubbles bursting over my tongue. Technically speaking, I'm too young to drink, but he knows that, doesn't he?

And besides... this man is not overly troubled by the law. His dealings on the black market are notorious.

He feeds me the cake last. We cut it together, his chest warm and hard at my back. His hand engulfs mine as I clutch the knife, and he guides it gently through the icing.

I barely notice. His cock is pressed against the base of my

spine, rigid and insistent. I bite my lip, a shiver traveling over my skin, and he drags his nose up the side of my throat.

"Do you feel that?" he murmurs, inhaling the scent of my hair. I give a wobbly nod. "That's what you do to me, princess. You drive me out of my goddamn mind. You make me an *animal*."

A shudder rolls through me, all the way to my core, and I spin in his arms, the knife clattering to the floor behind me. He smirks down at me, lifting a finger coated in icing, then presses it between my lips.

I open for him easily, moaning around his thick finger. I slurp and suck all the icing off, until the sugary taste is gone and I'm still sliding my lips up and down his knuckles. He stands still as a statue, letting me drive myself wild, his body vibrating with tension.

I swirl my tongue around the tip of his finger.

He snaps.

"Out!" he bellows, spinning to yell toward the kitchen. "Everyone out!" When he turns back to me, his eyes are burning. "I know you like an audience, don't you darling? You loved hearing those cars pass by earlier. But *no one* will see when I pop your cherry. That sight is only for me."

I nod in a daze as waiters and kitchen staff rush past, heads down as they hurry for the lobby. When the last footsteps echo across the marble and the door slams closed, the Fox rakes his eyes over me.

He nods. "Let's begin."

Garrett

My new bride is a needy thing. She's been glassy-eyed and pink-cheeked since the driveway, squeezing her thighs together when she thinks I'm not looking. Tendrils of her hair have escaped her elaborate updo, hanging down to tickle her bare shoulders, and her breath keeps catching at the sensation.

Poor angel. She's so desperate for it, she's climbing out of her skin.

I might find it amusing, but the humbling fact is that I'm just as bad. My skin is hot and oversensitive. I feel every brush of my clothes, every breeze floating through an open window. *She* made me like this, with those bee-stung lips and her heaving chest.

I've got her. I'll make these feelings go away.

Part of me wants to grab her tiny waist and lift her onto the table. To let the remains of our dinner stain her white gown, painting our passions over the fabric.

I won't do that. Perhaps it's foolish, perhaps it's wishful thinking, but I want her to look back on our wedding with fondness. This dress will be a keepsake, and I want her to treasure it, not stain it with gravy.

That doesn't mean I won't rip it.

That's what seamstresses are for.

"Come." I grasp her slender wrist, tugging her out of the dining room. More than anything, I want to take her to the master bathroom and watch her bathe, surrounded by moonlit mountains. But she cowed away from that—clearly, she doesn't want to bathe when I'm near. She doesn't trust me.

Yet. If it's my life's work, I will earn this angel's trust.

I take her to our bedroom instead, pulling her through the doorway. I avoided it on the tour, not trusting myself, but I'm glad now when I see her round eyes. The four poster bed stands in the center of the room, surrounded by plush, hand-woven rugs, and the balcony door is open. Delicate white drapes flutter in the breeze, and the room smells of pine. A fire crackles in the hearth.

She wets her lips, stepping toward the bed. Her bare toes poke out from under her hem, and I can't stand it anymore.

I've waited long enough.

And she makes a beast out of me.

I growl, scooping her up from behind and tossing her down on the mattress. She bounces on it, limbs flying, her small breasts bobbing beneath her gown.

I stand at the foot of the bed, flicking my shirt buttons open one by one. She watches my chest get bared with hungry eyes. Her small hands grip the covers, twisting them in her grip.

"Do you know what a husband and wife do, sweet thing?"

She bites her lip. Lifts one shoulder.

"Answer me."

"M-maybe," she gasps out. "I've read, um. Read some books."

I quirk an eyebrow, sliding the shirt off my shoulders.

"What kind of books?"

She shrugs again, squirming on the bed as I step closer. I move faster than a cobra, yanking her by the ankle. She's face down with the gown flipped over her back, her ass bared to the air before she can take a breath.

My palm cracks down on her ass cheek, sharp and firm. She moans, wriggling on the mattress.

"I told you to answer me," I say casually, rubbing the blushing pink patch of skin. "Are you trying to make me angry?"

"Maybe," she hisses into the bed covers, and I can't help my savage grin.

Yes. My sweet angel and I like the same games. She doesn't even fully know it yet; she's acting purely on her instincts. But she's bold, too, never mind how shy she seems—pushing her ass higher and wiggling it from side to side.

Crack.

I smack the other cheek, rubbing it after again. She moans brokenly, shaking her head and burrowing her face into the covers.

Well. That won't do.

I won't let her hide away and pretend this isn't real. I flip her over easily, smirking at her red cheeks and disheveled hair.

"What books?" I ask again.

She blinks at me hazily. "Um. Novels from my sister. Naughty books."

I freeze, ice sliding through my veins, but I force my hands to keep rubbing over her legs.

From her sister?

I *knew* something was off.

This isn't Lily Mountford.

There's a liar in my bed. A beautiful liar. She and her father have made a fool out of me. Violence and rage surge in my chest, and I grind my teeth together. But my hands on her stay steady. Smooth and gentle.

I won't *hurt* her, however badly she's hurt me.

Surely she knows this ruse can't last? I flip her over again while I think, letting my horror and confusion play over my face. I spank her ass a few more times, but there's no heat in it. I tug her skirt back down and crawl over her, kneading her shoulders instead.

There are knots in her slender muscles. I tease them out, listening to her breathy moans as my world crumbles down around me.

She knows her trick won't last.

She never planned to stay.

My beautiful liar plans to run.

My thoughts spin wildly, my heart racing so fast I'm surprised it doesn't burst clean out of my chest. By the time I've worked the last knot from her shoulders, I know what I must do.

She'll hate me for it.

I'll do it anyway.

She cannot leave.

Some lonely, hopeful part of me still thinks there's a chance. That I could make her love me. Could make her *want* to stay.

It's foolish, but I indulge that hope. I duck my head and bite the nape of her neck.

"Oh, please!"

She writhes beneath me, bucking her hips up, seeking friction. What was Lily's twin sister called again?

There was no name. Only that *lie.* 'Deceased'.

40

"Do you want me, baby?" I ask, desperation making my voice rough.

"Please, please, please," she sobs. "I need you inside me, F-Fox."

"It's Garrett," I snap. Are we both to be nameless? I tear her gown open, buttons be damned. Our wedding is no perfect memory. "Names are important, aren't they, *Lily?*"

She falters under me, and I lick a stripe up the length of her spine. Her back muscles twitch as I go, and she begins to move again.

"Call me angel instead. Please, Garrett."

God, I should end this charade. Call her out on her lies. But hearing my name in her husky voice…

I cannot deny this woman anything. Not even when it breaks my heart.

My teeth scrape over her shoulder.

"*Angel.* My angel." She moans again, bucking against me. I won't—I can't—deny her any longer. I bunch her skirt around her waist and squeeze her ass cheeks in my hands.

I've been picturing this moment all day, and in every vision, we were face to face.

Not now. She'll know her game is up the second she looks in my eyes. So I squeeze her ass cheeks, prying them apart and smacking them in turn.

Her flesh is already slick and quivering when I trace a fingertip over her slit. I circle her clit, smirking at her strangled moan, then drift back to her pussy.

I slide one knuckle deep. Two knuckles. Her pussy is so fucking wet and tight, constricting around me. If it strangles my *finger* like this—

I blow out a breath and stroke her walls.

I won't go any deeper. I won't risk taking her cherry with anything but my cock. And I barely need to stroke her at all before she's ready for me, hoarse-voiced and begging.

"Please, Garrett. Please, don't tease, please, please, I'm yours. Take me, take me, take me..."

She trails off, face buried in the bed covers. I kneel up behind her, yanking my belt loose. I draw my cock out and give it two rough strokes.

She gasps as I gather her wrists and hold them at the small of her back. They're dwarfed in one of my hands, the other winding in her hair and pulling her head back with a tug.

"Show me what you can do, baby." I push into her opening, groaning at the stretch. Her pussy clutches me, drawing me deeper, deeper, and I slide forward inch by inch. "Still with me, baby?" I grit out. She nods, her head swaying drowsily in my grip.

"Uh-huh."

"Does it feel good? Do you like my cock in your pussy?"

"Feels so good," she whispers. "I want *more*."

I snap my hips, thrusting deeper, and break past her barrier. God, her moans *wreck* me. She's loud and unselfconscious, no shame tingeing her pleasure. She begs for every inch of me, and when we're sealed flush together, she sighs and rolls her head on her neck.

She glances back at me, a glint in those emerald eyes.

"What are you waiting for? Show my pussy it's yours."

I growl, lunging forward, pounding her into the mattress. I'm being rough, way too rough, but she *loves* it, the little hellcat. She scrabbles at the bed covers, her limbs thrashing, urging me on with every moan from her pretty mouth. She cries out like she's in heat, begging for more and more, sighing happily with every crack of my palm on her ass.

"Do you like the pain, sweet thing?"

"Yes."

I lift her hips higher, holding her above the bed. I thrust into her at a punishing angle, rivulets of sweat trickling down my chest. Her torn gown is bunched and twisted on the bed; her braids are in ruins. I fist her hair tighter, yanking her head back, and her mouth drops open as she groans at the ceiling.

"You. Are. Mine."

I punctuate every word with a hard thrust of my cock. The breath leaves her body with each of my thrusts, and the enormous bed itself scrapes over the floor.

"I'm yours," she babbles, her head lolling as the spasms begin in her core. I feel her orgasm coming long before it hits, the tremors flickering through her muscles. Then her pussy clamps down, clenching on my cock, pleasure shuddering through her in waves. She cries out, her throat torn, and I knead her ass cheek, riding her as she comes.

When she collapses forward, I follow her down, plastering myself to her damp back. I lick at the moisture on her skin as I thrust three more times before burying myself deep and bursting inside her.

"Fuck." Even now, she's twitching around my cock. I come and come like a fire hose, painting her inner walls. A thought flashes across my mind—that she might get pregnant with my child—and I thrust impossibly deeper, filling her to the brim.

Let her be pregnant, I pray silently. Selfishly. *Let her be tied to me forever. My beautiful liar.*

At last, I pull out and roll off her, gathering her into my arms. Her makeup is smeared and her hair is wild. She looks like she's been dragged backwards through a hedge.

She's gorgeous.

"Don't leave me," I mutter, rubbing her back as she falls asleep against my chest. "Don't you dare leave me, angel."

Her soft breaths are the only reply.

God. I'm fucking ruined.

Nora

‿◠◡◠‿

I wait until the Fox—until *Garrett*—falls asleep, his deep breaths tickling the hairs on my neck. Only then do I peek out from under an eyelid, checking his face.

Crap. He's so handsome. Even now, in sleep, a scowl is etched on his forehead. I fight the urge to smooth it with my fingertip, wriggling gently out from under his arm.

His breath hitches. I freeze, halfway out the bed. Then he rolls over and lets out a sigh.

Good. This is good. I try to tell myself so, even as tears slide down my cheeks. I shouldn't feel like my heart is breaking in my chest over a man I only met today.

He doesn't even know who I am.

He doesn't want me. He wants Lily.

And I can't be here when he realizes. I couldn't bear to watch him turn me away. It would break me forever.

Better to get ahead of this. To slip out when I can, and stick with the plan: freedom. Life. *Adventure.*

Never mind the ache in my chest.

Never mind my churning stomach.

My wedding dress is ruined—not that it would be much use for running away. I tiptoe to another door in the bedroom, and pry open Garrett's walk-in closet.

I dress quickly, picking clothes for practicalities' sake. A pair of his jeans, belted at my waist and rolled at the ankles. Two thick pairs of socks, since there's no way his shoes will fit me and I'm not wearing heels through the mountains.

A long-sleeved t-shirt. A black sweater and an overcoat.

A glance in the mirror shows that I look freaking insane.

With my smudged makeup, wild hair and oversized clothes, I look like a little girl playing dress up in Daddy's closet.

The thought makes me shiver, but I tuck it away.

It's no use. I have to leave.

I pick my way across the bedroom, forcing myself to keep walking and not look at the man on the bed. If I look, I'll crumble. I'll confess everything and beg to stay.

I can't do that. It will hurt too much when he says no. When he looks at me with disgust in his eyes.

The bedroom door swings open easily, and I pad silently down the hall in my thick socks. I glance up and down, wracking my tired brain, trying to remember my way through this house.

Left, I think. Left and a little way along the corridor, then down the big, sweeping stairs.

My chest lightens a fraction when I find my way. I'm not *so* useless, then. Not like my father used to say. If I can just find my way out, get into the mountains and start working my way toward the city...

Then what?

I have no money. Nothing to sell. My eyes flutter closed,

and I breathe through a sharp pain in my chest.

I hate this. I hate doing this to him, but it's my only hope. I pluck one of Garrett's sculptures off a mantelpiece in the lobby. It's likely worth thousands at least—enough for me to start my new life.

"I'm sorry," I whisper, reaching for the door. "I'm so sorry."

"I should hope so."

I gasp and whirl around. Garrett leans against the wall in the shadows. He's watching me, scowling at the statue gripped in my hands.

There's no way out of this. No lie he'd ever believe.

I crept out when he was sleeping, dressed in his clothes and stole his artwork, his precious art—

"Garrett." I open and close my mouth, searching for words, but they don't come. His expression darkens. I squeak, spinning back to the door, but the statue slips from my numb fingertips. It shatters against the marble floor, shards flying in all directions. Garrett yells something, but I'm already running.

My heel feels hot as I fly down the gravel driveway. The lanterns lining the path stretch and warp my shadow, so that a fun house version of me flees on either side. Behind me, Garrett bellows from the house, but I sprint into the night.

My heel is *burning*. The gravel digs into my feet, makes me wince and gasp, but my heel is beginning to throb. Suddenly, pain lances hot through my foot and I cry out, staggering to the side.

Strong arms catch me, steady me, and I'm lifted into the air. I half expect Garrett to throttle me, but he cradles me against his chest. He dressed in gray sweatpants and a dark t-shirt to follow me down to the lobby, but his feet are bare against the gravel.

"Angel!" He yells, trying to stop me struggling. "Fucking hell, stop it! You've hurt yourself."

I go limp in his arms, panting from exhaustion.

"I'm not your angel," I mutter. He stiffens around me. I screw my eyes shut and force myself to keep speaking. There's nothing else for it now. "I'm not who you think I am. I'm not Lily Mountford."

Garrett huffs, turning around and striding back up his driveway.

"No shit. You already told me."

"I did?" Am I going insane? Surely I'd remember a conversation about that.

"Yeah." He smirks at me, the shadows cast by the lanterns dancing across his face. "When you were out-of-your-mind needy for my cock."

I blink, heat rushing to my cheeks. God, how humiliating. But—

"If you already know, why are you taking me back inside?"

Garrett rolls his eyes.

"You hurt your foot. Stepped on a shard from that statue."

I glance down at my dangling foot, and sure enough, crimson blood is blooming over the heel. It's soaked through two thick socks already, and another wave of pain lances through me at the thought.

I whimper, clutching at Garrett's t-shirt. He shifts me in his arms, cradling me closer.

"Hush, baby. We'll take a look. I'll fix it for you, I promise."

Baby? Hope blooms in my chest. Wild, impossible hope.

I wet my lips, my arms tightening around his neck.

"I'm sorry for running," I whisper. "I didn't think you'd still want me." There's so much more to tell him—about my father, about being locked away—but his face already softens. He gazes down at me, eyes burning, and his voice shakes when he speaks.

"I'll always want you, angel. You're *mine*."

Joy breaks over my face, stretching my lips into a wide smile. I squeal and snuggle into him closer.

"It's Nora," I tell him, nipping at his earlobe.

He snorts, cracking his palm against my ass.

"Makes sense. Naughty Nora."

He carries me inside. Lays me gently on the sofa. Fetches the first aid kit and patches my cut. Garrett fusses over me like a priceless treasure. Like he's a teddy bear, not an internationally-renowned art dealer.

I watch him, and I must have cartoon hearts in my eyes, because every time he glances up, he smiles. His eyes crease at the corners, warmth spreading over his cold features, and my chest aches at the sight.

"Do you really still want me?"

He grips my ankle, glaring from his knees. "*Always.*"

I sigh and collapse back on the cushions, tossing my arms over my head. This can't be real, this must be some sort of dream, no one can be this lucky.

"Garrett?" I ask. His palms slide up my thighs. He reaches my waist and tugs at the belt. "Why do people call you the Fox?"

He huffs a laugh, flicking the button open on his jeans and dragging them down my legs. I lift my hips to help, warmth already pooling in my core, my bandaged wound long forgotten.

"Because I made my fortune squeezing into tight spaces." He

traces a line up my inner thigh, then cups my pussy in a strong, possessive grip. "Shall I show you?"

I nod so fast my teeth chatter, and his dark, smoky laugh thrills through my veins as he spreads my legs wide. He tests me with a finger, but I'm ready for him. Wet and aching.

This time, when he pushes his big cock inside me, we're face to face. His forehead drops onto mine, and he rocks his head back and forth as he pushes deeper, inch by inch. I prop myself up on my elbows and we watch together as the thick length of him vanishes inside me.

"See that, pretty girl?" Garrett fists my hair and tugs. "Your pussy was made to swallow my cock."

I nod, still watching hypnotized as he slides in and out of me. My juices shine on the flushed skin of his cock, and I reach down to rub a fingertip over his shaft.

Garrett hisses, grabbing my knees and folding my legs up and back, pounding into me so hard my teeth rattle. I moan and scrabble at his hips, his shoulders, pulling him closer, *harder*, and all the while he stares at me, his eyes dark.

"You will never leave me." The way he says it, it sounds like a promise.

Good thing I never want to.

I shake my head, biting my lip as he smacks my ass. Garrett likes me to reply out loud.

"Never," I gasp. "Never. I love you."

The words just slip out, and his hips falter. Heat flushes my cheeks, and I duck my head, so embarrassed, but he tips my chin back up.

"I love you." His eyes bore into mine. All the way into my *soul*. "I love you so fucking much, I can hardly stand it, Nora. You're mine. Fucking *mine*. And tomorrow..." he leans forward, tugging my bottom lip between his teeth. He speaks against my mouth. "Tomorrow, I'm going to find that fucking priest and marry you properly. The right names this time, huh, sweetheart?"

I nod and smile through my tears.

Yes. I want that. I want that so badly. I tip my head back and moan as he thrusts again, his cock plunging inside me.

I want everything he has to give me. His huge, hard cock. The crack of his palm. The obsessive light burning in his eyes.

His surname and his home.

A baby one day.

I'm his?

He's also *mine.*

Garrett

Five years later

I slam my car door shut, striding up the paved driveway toward the mansion.

Our mansion. My wife's. My family's.

How did I ever get so fucking lucky?

The early evening light casts a warm glow over the mountains. The huge glass windows sparkle, and the lobby is cool as I step inside.

I used to come home from business trips to silence. Perhaps a single staff member. Now, when I listen, I hear the whoops of our children playing in their room. The nanny's soft voice murmurs to them, calms them a little, and I smile.

That means I have my wife to myself.

It doesn't take me long to find her. She's in her favorite place in the mansion—the room she goes to when she wants to relax. I push the master bathroom door open, savoring the steady reveal of her bare arms draped along the stone bathtub.

I close the door behind me. Spin the lock. Only then does she glance back, her face brightening. Her scar shifts with the motion, but she doesn't cringe in embarrassment any more.

She knows she's the most beautiful woman I've ever seen.

"You're home!" She moves to stand up, but I hold up a palm.

"Wait." She settles back into the bubbly water, biting her lip. My Nora loves when I boss her around. It makes her so fucking wet. "Sit back," I tell her. "Wash your arms."

She does it slowly, putting on a show. I stroll around the side of the tub, glancing out at the mountains.

Anyone could walk past. Could glance up from their car.

Yes, my wife is a naughty girl.

"Your legs next," I rasp, my hungry gaze raking over her bare, soapy skin. She wriggles her toes against the rim of the bathtub, showing off her latest design. Marbled swirls of pale pink over cream.

My wife is an artist. An extraordinary talent. With a little investment, her nail art design company has become famous around the world.

It's all her. I just put in a little money. All the talent, all the vision—it's all Nora.

"Have you been a good girl?"

She nods, biting her lip. When I growl, a faint smile tugs at her lips. She likes to tease me like this. Make me spank the answers out of her. I stroll across the bathroom, hands in my pockets.

"Did you miss me, angel?"

She nods again, cheeks flushing. Yes, I know very well how badly she missed me. She tortured me with photos of her in tiny scraps of lace; she called me every night, pleading for me to get her off.

I did my best. I had her coming every night, clenching my jaw at her gasps down the phone.

I didn't come, though. I saved it all for her.

This is *my* revenge.

"Undo my belt." Her soapy fingers scrabble at my clothes. She gets my cock out before I can even ask, wrapping both hands around it.

"What do I do next?" she asks, feigning innocence. I smirk down at her, tugging her chin down. When I tap the head of my cock against her tongue, a shudder rolls through her.

Always so responsive, my wife. So needy.

She moans as I thrust between her lips.

I cradle her head in my hands, fingers playing in her caramel hair. She gazes up at me so lovingly as I fuck her mouth.

"This is what you wanted, isn't it, sweetheart?" She moans in agreement, her tongue flicking over my cock. "You wanted my come poured down your pretty throat."

Her eyelids drift closed, one hand dropping back beneath the water. The frenzied movement of her arm disturbs the water; makes it slosh onto the tiles.

I don't stop. Neither does she. We're lost in our own world, me fucking her mouth and her fucking her own fingers.

I'll give her my cock later. Over and over again. Enough to make up for all the days apart. But for now, I thrust into that pretty little mouth, claiming her the way she craves.

Rough. Primal. Desperate.

All the things she makes me feel.

"Angel," I groan, emptying myself into her mouth. She sucks my come down greedily, slurping just for show. As soon as I'm finished, I yank her up by the elbow, bending her over to grip the rim of the bathtub.

My tongue plunges between her folds, and I eat her pussy in a frenzy, grinding my whole face between her legs. By the time she comes, she's *all* over me, and I nip at her quivering ass cheek.

"Good girl," I huff, catching my breath. I trace an idle circle over her clit. "Good girl."

Upstairs, our children are laughing. Playing. The mountains stretch around us on all sides, painted golden.

My wife sits back down in the bathwater, giggling as she wipes at my face.

Yeah.

I'm the luckiest fucking bastard in the world.

My tongue pops between her lips, and I can feel her

I feel her grabbing my whole face between her legs. If the

time she comes she will over me, and I wipe her quivering

ass, then,

Good girl," I tell, reaching up, proud. I arse and then rub

over her. "Good girl."

I raise her chin once more, sighing. Phving. "The mountains

shift and undulate on all sides satisfied. Golden—

My wife sits back down to the tank water, laughing as she

wipes at my face.

Yeah.

I'm the luckiest man in the world.

II

Stolen Bride

Lily

I lean out of Nora's tower window, watching the row of cars pull out of the driveway. I wave as big as I can even though there's no way my sister can see me, my eyes wet and my heart lodged tight in my throat.

She's doing this for me. Heading out into the big wide world, letting our father trade her away to his business rival in a sham of a marriage. It was her idea to take my place—she begged me to let her do it, saying it was her only chance of escape—but guilt and shame still slosh in my stomach.

We spent hours this morning perfecting our ruse, painting her scar with make-up and curling her hair just like mine, and my heart sank another inch for every minute of it. Right now, watching the line of shiny black cars carry my twin sister away, the poor, battered organ is somewhere near my belly button.

"Don't be scared," Nora had whispered as I brushed mascara into her lashes, my chin wobbling with unshed tears. "It's all a trick. One quick kiss at the altar, and I'll slip away before the Fox knows it." She took my hands in hers, squeezing. "I *want*

59

this, Lily. This is it. He might not know it, but the Fox is my chance to be free."

The Fox. I think of the man who was meant to be my husband, and a shudder passes through me. He's notorious. Driven and severe.

God, I hope Nora is okay. I suppose after spending the last eleven years locked away in this tower, *anything* must seem like a better option.

Even marrying a complete stranger.

At least the Fox is handsome. Famously so. He's one of the city's most sought after bachelors, with his clean-cut features, elegant taste, and bottomless bank accounts. Plenty of girls would have killed to be in my position, promised to the mysterious art dealer.

Not me. There's only one man I want, and he is standing six feet behind me with his arms crossed, blocking Nora's bedroom door.

My bodyguard.

Reuben.

The man I cry out for in my sleep.

Of course, to Reuben I'm just an annoying kid. His employer's spoiled daughter. He watches over me, guards me closely, but in the three long years he's known me, he's never really *seen* me.

You know, as more than an object.

As a woman.

"Be careful," he grumbles now as I lean further out the open window. I ignore him, pushing up on my toes to watch the line of cars as they pull out of the driveway—

Reuben huffs, stomping across the bedroom. He catches me by the arm, tugging me back inside and shoving the window closed with a thud.

"Do you want your father to see you?" he snaps, crowding me back into the center of the room. "Your little trick will be over before it's begun."

I scoff, crossing my arms just like he always does.

"Why do you care? You should *want* me to get caught. My father's going to kill you for not warning him, you know."

Reuben shrugs, supremely unconcerned.

"I'm a bodyguard. Not a babysitter."

"Oh? Is that the only reason?" I raise my eyebrows, watching him closely. When Reuben went along with our twin swap, sneaking me into Nora's tower at dawn, I could hardly believe it. He could get fired for this, or so much worse. Our father is a cruel man.

But a part of me, just a tiny part, got to thinking... got to hoping...

Maybe Reuben didn't want me to marry the Fox, either.

Maybe he thinks there's someone better for me, too.

I hold my breath as I wait for him to answer. He glowers down at me, his rough features creased into a scowl, and I swear his eyes heat as they skate quickly over my body. I'm in Nora's yoga pants and vest top, just like she's now wearing my wedding gown. My skin flushes under his gaze, a knot twisting in my abdomen, and I sway an inch toward him in a trance.

"Yes," Reuben clips out, stepping back. I fall back on my heels, disappointment sour in my mouth. "That's all it is. Don't get a big head."

Hurt ripples through my chest. Is it so big-headed to think my gruff bodyguard might want me too? Is it so damn unlikely? I pluck at Nora's yoga pants, glaring at the floor between us.

"Got it," I mutter. "Message received."

"Lily—"

He reaches for me, frowning, but it's my turn to dance out of reach. I turn on my heel and stride out of the bedroom, back to Nora's cramped living room with her tiny sofa and scuffed coffee table.

It's nothing like my palatial suite. My twin sister's life has been the opposite of mine, and all because of a stupid scar marring her beauty. I throw myself down onto the sofa, chewing on my thumbnail in a way that would make Nora cringe.

I have no right to complain. Not really. Not when my sister's had it so much worse; not when she's going out there right now to take my place.

But I can't help the pain and longing that swirl in my chest, making my heart throb the way it always does around Reuben.

I keep my face blank. Stare at the wall and count my breaths. Focus on Nora, and on the storm heading my way as soon as my father discovers our trick.

Not Reuben. Not the way my hairs stand on end in his presence, and blood pumps hot and throbbing between my legs. Not his clean, masculine scent, or the creak of the floorboards beneath his big, manly form. Not the way my breath catches every time I feel his gaze on me.

He clears his throat. I throw Reuben a perfect, staged smile. It's fine. I know he could never want me.

* * *

Perhaps in another life, I might have stood a chance with Reuben. If we'd met when I was legally an adult, instead of sixteen. If I could have charmed him in a cafe somewhere, instead of being handed over like some kind of troublesome puppy by my father.

I could have flirted. Brushed a casual palm over his shoulder. Seen his eyes darken with promise.

I'd have let him take me home—back to wherever Reuben goes when he's not here.

He knows every single thing about me. I don't even know where he lives, and the thought of his mystery home is the most agonizing riddle. Is he neat? What color are his walls? Does he have a garden; bookshelves; a fancy kitchen?

"Do you like cooking?"

My question breaks the silence. Reuben glances over from his station by the door, his hands clasped behind his back. His white shirt stretches over his broad chest, the buttons straining, and I *desperately* want them to give up the battle.

I bet he has chest hair. My mouth waters just thinking about it. He's got this thick, manly scruff around his jaw, and I just *know* that it's dusted over his body, too.

I want to rake my nails over it. I want to lick him from hip to collarbone.

"What? Cooking? Why do you ask?"

I roll my eyes. "To gather blackmail material. Because I'm *interested*, you doofus."

"Doofus?" Reuben's mouth twitches. "I haven't been called that before."

"I bet you've been called a lot worse."

He chuckles, the sound smoky. "You bet right."

Oh god. I squeeze my thighs together on the sofa. Oh god,

oh god. I spend most of my waking hours around this man—I have done for the last three years. Surely at some point I should have gotten used to him? Should have been inoculated to his presence?

"You didn't answer the question." I sound hoarse. Reuben cocks his head, regarding me. His gaze rakes over my features, dropping down my body then back up.

"Yeah," he says eventually. "I like cooking. When I get the chance."

"Right." I screw up my face. "I'm kind of a time suck, huh?" He's here every morning before I wake up, and stays long after I'm tucked away in bed again. Every day of the week, for three years straight.

Reuben lifts one shoulder. "I don't mind."

It's the closest thing he's ever said to a compliment. I stifle a smile, turning back to the bare wall. I don't know how Nora spent eleven straight years in this room without going insane. I've been here for two hours and I want to chew on the coffee table.

The sound of car engines rumbling down the driveway make me shoot to my feet. I suck in shallow breaths, suddenly panicked, but a warm hand steadies my elbow.

"Lily." Reuben ducks his head. Makes me meet his eyes. "It's going to be okay." The pad of his thumb swoops back and forth over my bare arm. Back and forth. It anchors me.

I swallow and nod, even though Reuben can't know that. My father is capable of terrible things. And he'll see this as the worst kind of betrayal—I've set my sister free and shamed him to his business rival, all in one go.

Reuben gives me a little shake. I stare into his hazel eyes and settle down. My breaths come slower. Calmer.

"Nothing bad will happen to you," he murmurs. "I promise."

Nothing bad will appear to you, he murmurs. "I promise.

Reuben

꧁ᥫᨕ꧂

If I had my way, Lily wouldn't even be here right now. We'd have skipped out the second her father left the mansion, and we'd be heading out of state with new names.

It can't be that way, though. Lily... she trusts me to protect her. To keep her safe.

And if I had her all to myself, out there in the big wide world... I don't know how long I could keep my hands to myself.

Just the thought of it sickens me. My weakness. My shame. The way I've wanted this sweet, perfect girl since only weeks after she turned eighteen. Before that, I longed for her too, but not in the same way. I wanted to care for her. Cherish her and make her smile.

Now I want to do other things to her.

Filthy things.

It doesn't take a genius to see how wrong that is. Lily is young. Inexperienced. She's practically a princess, and I'm a big fucking brute almost twice her age. I don't deserve to breathe the same air as her as it is, but if I put my hands on her?

I'd rather die than break her trust that way.

Even if it's killing me day by day. Even if I beat my cock to thoughts of her every night until it's raw.

Residual lust still coils in my belly as I stride through the halls to meet her father. She has that effect on me. She doesn't even have to try. Just being near her lights a fire in my blood.

Just get this over with, I tell myself as I pass rows of priceless paintings in ornate frames. If it were possible, I think Mountford would frame his daughter and hang her up on that wall, too.

An object. That's how he sees her. A possession to flaunt and trade.

If Lily and Nora didn't come up with their twin swap, the wedding would still not have happened. I may have sworn to keep my hands off Lily, but I would tear the limbs off another man before I watch him marry my girl.

This is better. Poor Nora gets out, Lily stays safe from men, and she gets to keep her lifestyle. All the riches and opportunities that her father can give her. One day, she'll make her own way, but until then...

Well. Mountford's a prick, but at least she wants for nothing. That's more than I can offer her.

My boots sink into the long, plush rug as I near Mountford's office. Something crashes against the wall, the sound of breaking glass echoing down the hallway.

I roll my eyes, shoulders relaxed. A tantrum, then. Mountford is a child. And sure enough, when I stand in his office doorway, he snarls and throws a paperweight at my head.

I catch it easily. No power behind the throw. And when I

raise my eyebrow, Mountford shrinks back.

"You should have told me," he mutters, flinging himself into his desk chair. "The Fox will ruin me for this. He won't want damaged goods."

"Perhaps he'll see Nora's true value." I stroll into the room, hands in my pockets. Mountford squints at me, trying to find the insult.

There is none. While Nora has never stirred the same feelings in me as Lily, I pity the girl. And I admire her strength.

I'm glad she found a way out, even if it costs me now. Even if she weren't saving Lily, I wouldn't have stood in her way.

"Is there something you want to say to me?" I give Mountford a fair chance. I wait with my face blank and shoulders relaxed. He'd be within his rights to fire me, to rant at me, but he doesn't.

Coward.

No, he'd rather blame his girls. The two people he has true power over.

"This won't stand," Mountford mutters, half to himself and half to me, stabbing a letter opener into his desk. "If she won't marry the Fox, she'll learn. There are plenty more who'd have her."

I stiffen, muscles tensing.

"You mean to marry Lily off? For the sake of it?" I say, voice low.

It takes every ounce of control not to lunge forward and choke the life from this weasel. Mountford smirks at me, like I'll enjoy this too. His wedding tux is creased, sagging from his shoulders, and sweat shines on his forehead. With his thinning dark hair, threaded with gray, and his down-turned lips, it's a wonder he fathered such beauties.

"What can I say?" He grins at me with sickly enjoyment. "Lily clearly needs a firm hand. And I've had offers before..." He trails off and licks his lips.

My stomach lurches, my skin flushing hot.

"What offers?"

Mountford leans over his desk, his chair creaking. His eyes are bright and fevered, his cheeks flushed with excitement and rage.

"Art isn't the only thing bought and sold on the black market."

I hum and nod, murmuring vague responses, but a roaring sound fills my ears. It takes all my military training to keep myself in check. To fake agreement. To play along.

This way, I'm in the loop. I'm part of his plans. He trusts me with his sick intentions for his daughter.

Mountford is blind as well as cruel. I'd tear his heart out and eat it before I let him sell Lily.

* * *

Her shoulder is delicate under my palm. I shake her gently, keeping my gaze fixed on her sleeping face. Her caramel hair fans out across the pillow, and her chest rises and falls with each breath. Her limbs are tangled in the bed sheets, one bare ankle peeking through the covers, but I don't let myself look. Not for more than a second, anyway.

I shake her harder, growling.

"Lily. Wake up, princess. It's time to go."

"Hm?"

She's adorably sleepy. She wrinkles her nose, huffing at

being woken in the middle of the night. When she props herself up on one elbow, squinting at my shape in the darkness, there's no hint of fear in the set of her shoulders. Her body is pliant, warm from sleep, and her night shirt is slipping off one arm. It's one of those old fashioned satin ones with the collar and the little row of buttons.

My cock swells in my black pants, pressing against my zipper.

"Reuben?" she mumbles, rubbing the heel of her palm in her eye. My breath rasps in and out of my chest, and I swear the steady thump of my heart is so loud it must echo down the hall.

I've never come to Lily like this, in the dark depths of her bedroom, when the rest of the mansion is asleep. An owl hoots outside her window and she glances outside, the moonlight dancing over the planes of her face.

When she looks back at me, she's frowning. I can just make out the little shadow on her forehead in the dark.

"This is a dream," she murmurs. "You're not really here."

I swallow hard. "It's not a dream. Come on, princess. Time to get up."

"Nope." She stifles a yawn. "That doesn't make sense. You normally sleep at home, wherever *that* is." She rolls her head, like her neck is stiff, and sits all the way upright. Before I have time to react, her arms slide around my neck and her hot mouth nibbles at my earlobe.

"I've had this dream before," she breathes, pressing a kiss to my throat. "It's one of my favorites."

I should move. Push her away. But I stay frozen, my mind bright white and empty as she scoots closer, pressing her body against mine. Her nipples pebble under her thin nightshirt, and I feel them drag over my chest. Her mouth is hot on my skin, her little tongue darting out to taste the hollow of my collarbone.

A shudder runs through me, all the way down to my boots.

"Lily," I snap, grabbing her shoulders and jerking her back. She blinks up at me, eyes wide, the sleepiness clearing from her face in the moonlight. Embarrassment and bitterness take its place, and she shoves away from me with a gasp. She crowds all the way back against her headboard, like she can't get far enough away.

I straighten up, gut clenching. She's awake. No need to loom over her like a fucking creep. Not when she's clearly half out of her mind.

"Get up. We need to go."

Lily chokes out a laugh, twisting the covers in her hands.

"I'm not going anywhere with you."

Impatience rushes through me and makes me clench my jaw. There's no damn time for this, not tonight. Lily can be a handful on a good day, and god knows I love that about her. But if we're going to slip away, get out of this messed up house before her father wakes, she needs to listen for once.

Listen, and obey.

"Up." My voice is low and quiet, but the command snaps through the still night air. Lily sucks in a gasp, and her legs squeeze together beneath her bed sheets.

Yeah. I figured she might be like that.

She opens her mouth to argue again, but I hold up a palm. She freezes, lips parted and chest heaving.

"You're coming with me," I tell her quietly. "Whether you like it or not. I don't have time to explain, so you just have to do as you're told. Can you do that?"

Her breaths are coming in quick pants, and she's practically squirming on the mattress. I'd bet a year's salary that when she stands up, there will be a wet spot on the sheets.

Turns out bratty Lily likes to be bossed around.

Fuck.

I adjust my pants, holding her gaze.

Lily wets her lip, her eyes dropping to my belt then back up again. Then she slams her mouth closed and shakes her head, fire sparking in her eyes.

"Lily," I growl. She clenches fistfuls of the bed sheet, watching me with held breath. "I won't tell you again. *Up.*"

She throws off her covers, swinging her legs out of the bed, and lunges towards the bedroom door. I catch her up easily, slinging her over my shoulder, not batting an eye as she pounds at my back with her fists.

"Put me down!" she hisses, pummeling my ass. I snort, and that makes her even madder. "Reuben! I swear to god. I will *scream.*"

That stops me chuckling. If she wakes up the house, her father's security will come running. And if they take me out, there's no one left standing between Lily and her father's sick plans.

I drop her back on her feet, the sound muffled by the rug. She stumbles to the side, confused, and I grip her by the elbow.

"Listen to me." Fuck. I sound way too harsh. The arousal coursing through my blood is making me gruffer than usual. Mean and rough. "This isn't a game, Lily. You're not safe here. So shut the fuck up and let's go."

She yanks her arm free, backing up a step. The hurt from a few minutes is still there, flinty in her green eyes, and I wish I hadn't been so harsh pushing her away.

It wasn't *her* I was disgusted with, but she doesn't know that. And the humiliation is thick in her voice.

"Who says I'm safe with *you*?"

I snarl. What a fucking joke.

"I'm the *only* one you're safe with. I'd die for you, Lily."

She huffs. "Because it's your job." She shakes her head, staring out the window again. In the silvery moonlight, she looks exhausted. "It's not real if it's bought and paid for. Please, Reuben." Her shoulders slump. "Leave me alone. I don't want to go with you. Whatever my father's punishment is, I'll deal with it."

No. No, no, no.

Maybe—*maybe*—I could accept that if she weren't in danger. But there are sick fucks out there bidding on her virtue. Who want to own her, use her, *hurt* her. I don't give a shit what she wants in this moment. She doesn't understand.

Lily is *mine*. Mine to protect. Mine to die for.

And mine to beat my cock over. She's no one else's.

"You'd really scream?"

She raises her chin and nods. So fucking brave.

"Fine." I reach up and slide my tie out of its knot, tugging the strip of fabric out from beneath my collar. She watches me, eyes big as saucers. "I didn't want to do this, princess."

Lie. A dirty lie.

I spin her quickly before she can react, gagging her with the tie. Lily jerks back to herself, fighting and scrabbling, her shouts muffled by the fabric, but it's too late. I catch her wrists easily, casting around before snatching the belt of her bathrobe out of its loops.

I tie her wrists behind her back gently but firmly, hating myself for the way my cock swells even harder in my pants.

It's for her. To keep her safe. I'll explain everything, just as soon as we're beyond her father's reach. I tell her so too, my words hushed and hot, and she shivers when my lips brush the shell of her ear.

This should have gone differently. How did I get this so wrong? She was supposed to have time to pack some things; she was supposed to slip away willingly, with her little hand tucked in mine.

Instead, Lily fights me every step across the bedroom, until I give up and sling her over my shoulder again. She kicks and headbutts me as I stride through the mansion, keeping to the shadows. And when we slip out of the house into the night, her muffled cries are ragged behind my tie.

"You'll understand soon, princess," I croak. God, how many times have I dreamed of stealing her away like this?

Is this even truly for her?

Or am I acting out my own darkest fantasies?

No. I force myself to remember Mountford's words in his study. His plans for selling Lily to the highest bidder like some kind of exotic pet.

Perhaps I am a monster. A savage beast of a man, who has no business lusting over sweet young girls.

But unlike those bastards, I won't touch her. No matter how much my instincts roar for me to take her, to bend her over and sink my cock into her tight, wet heat.

Lily will be safe with me. I made her a promise, and I mean to keep it.

Even if it means taking her to a new home, then getting myself far, far away.

Lily

What. The hell. Is happening?

Reuben carries me easily, his breath not even coming harder at having a whole squirming body slung over one shoulder. I gnaw at the tie pulled between my teeth, shaking my head and yelling into the fabric, but it's no use. He's trussed me up good.

Part of me is so freaking excited. I can feel the ridges of his hard muscles beneath my body; can feel the sturdiness of his limbs as I kick and thrash. I'm helpless, completely at my bodyguard's mercy, and how many times have I had this fantasy?

Too many to count.

He opens the rear door to his car, parked in the shadows at the end of the driveway. I'm tossed unceremoniously onto the backseat, bouncing against the leather with splayed limbs and an indignant squawk. Reuben ducks his big head, squeezing his shoulders into the car and crowding in after me.

I still as his fingers find the gag, smoothing around to the knot in the tie. His chest is level with my face, his pecs heaving up and down, and more than anything I want that body pressing forward onto mine.

"Will you be quiet?" he asks, voice low. A shiver rolls through me and I nod, eyes fixed on his. Their hazel looks darker in the moonlight.

His big fingers are deft, untying the knot easily and sliding the tie out of my tangled hair. I suck in a deep breath to scream the whole mansion down, but Reuben curses and claps his hand over my mouth.

"Lily," he grits out. "Princess. Stop it. I told you, this isn't a game."

Isn't it?

Because ever since I turned eighteen, Reuben and I have been circling each other like cats.

We push each other, teasing and taunting. We nudge each other toward breaking point, each holding our breath to see if the other will snap. I take showers and 'forget' to close the bathroom door, meeting Reuben's dark eyes in the fogged up mirror. He pulls me around like a rag doll, tugging cardigans onto my cold shoulders and smirking at the way my pupils dilate.

This has been a long time coming. Hasn't it?

The memory of Reuben's expression in the bedroom as he pushed me away drifts across my mind. I still, my ragged breaths damp against his massive palm. Just the thought of that moment—his curled lip, the irritation and disgust flashing through his eyes—makes a hole yawn open in my chest.

So maybe it's not a game after all. Maybe this is real, somehow.

I slump back against the car window. Reuben watches me closely, then removes his hand. He reaches around me and unties my wrists as he talks, his fingers so gentle.

"I'll explain everything, princess. I promise. But we need to get away from here first, alright?"

I nod, miserable. I can't speak. For a wild, aching moment, I'd thought I had everything. I thought my bodyguard was as desperate for me as I am for him, and we were finally going to give in to our dark, primal love.

Instead, I'm running away under cover of darkness. Away from the only home I've ever known. For Reuben to really do this, the danger must be terrible.

He'll lose everything. His job, his good name. His safety.

My father will hunt him across the country for this. Surely he knows that?

I wet my lip, still transfixed by his gaze. When I speak, my voice is hoarse from screaming.

"I'll go. I understand now. But you can't come with me, Reuben."

He rears back, anger and possessiveness rippling across his face.

"Like fuck. I'm not sending you out there unprotected." His grip finds my bare ankle, his thumb rubbing at the bone like a worry bead. "You're *mine*."

He doesn't mean that the way I want him to. Reuben is possessive as hell, and guarding me is a point of pride. Somehow, knowing that is worse than if he never said those words at all. I want to stuff them back into his mouth, so that they won't play on a loop in my head when I can't sleep.

"Whatever punishment my father has planned—"

"It won't happen." Reuben's voice is thick with the promise of violence. "I'll burn his home, his world, his whole damn empire down first."

"What did he—"

"It *doesn't matter.*" I can hear Reuben's teeth grinding, and that more than anything clues me in. Whatever this is, it's bad. Unthinkable.

Worse than an arranged marriage to the Fox.

A new, depraved low.

I shiver, pressing back against the cold car window. Hurt and nausea roil in my stomach. I know that my father can be cruel, can be thoughtless, but he's always loved me. *Treasured* me. Called me his little girl.

I guess that's over. And all because I helped my twin sister escape; because I didn't want to marry a strange man.

I wrap my arms around myself, suddenly aware that I only have a thin nightshirt to protect me from the cool air. Reuben grunts, his eyes dropping to my hard nipples pushing against the fabric. Then he's gone, ducking out of the car, his boots crunching on the gravel.

The trunk slams, and a blanket lands on my legs. It's rough and scratchy, smelling like mothballs. Reuben shuts the passenger door with a thud, and I tug the blanket up my body.

The car rocks under his weight. He meets my eyes in the rear view mirror.

"Lily. Seat belt."

I clip it in place, mouth dry, and only then does he begin to drive. I crane my neck, peering out of the rear window as the mansion disappears from view.

The only home, the only *family* I've ever known.

I tug the blanket over my head and muffle my sobs.

* * *

We drive for what feels like an eternity, the car rocking with dips in the road. After I've cried myself hoarse, when I'm dried out and exhausted, I pull the blanket back off my head.

Reuben watches me in the mirror, his face unreadable. I huff and stare out of the window instead, watching the ocean crash against the cliffs below the road. Seabirds wheel overhead in the pink tinge of dawn, and the water is steel gray in the morning light.

For the first time in my life, I don't want Reuben's eyes on me. The reminder is too painful right now.

He's the only good thing left in my universe. There's Nora, of course, but god knows when I'll see my twin sister again.

Reuben is my rock. He has been since the day we met. He's the center of my galaxy; the point that I orbit around.

And he's risking everything for me out of a sense of duty. It's so hollow and pointless, I could scream.

When my stomach growls loud enough to hear over the engine, Reuben pulls off the coast road into the parking lot for a diner. It's small and modest, but the blue painted walls are clean and the windows sparkle. Reuben opens my car door and I nearly topple out, his hands catching me easily.

He crouches and frowns at my rumpled nightshirt. With my rat's nest hair, I must look like I escaped from an asylum.

"We should have packed you some clothes."

I snort. "Yeah, no shit."

He grins at me, eyes twinkling as the sea breeze tugs his hair. A plain back sweater hugs his chest, and his dark jeans are faded at the knee. He looks so freaking handsome when he smiles, my heart flips over in my chest.

"I guess I got carried away," he murmurs, and it's the closest sign I've had that he enjoyed it too.

Stealing me away. Tying me up and throwing me over his shoulder.

How can I make that happen again?

I reach out to his face—I just want to scratch my nails over his beard—but he's already standing and striding away round the car. He comes back immediately, dropping a gym bag on the bare stone of the parking lot.

"It's all clean." He scrubs the back of his head, embarrassed. "It won't fit, but it'll cover you up, at least."

"What needs covering?" I toss the blanket off my legs and stretch them out in the cool air. He jerks his head around, face thunderous, but we're all alone. His eyes turn back to me, hungry and dark.

I wish.

This is the problem: Reuben plays along with me, but he doesn't really *want* me. Not truly.

Not outside of our games. Not the way I want him.

He crouches and tugs the gym bag's zipper open. A worn gray sweatshirt lands on my lap, along with a pair of black sweatpants and thick white socks. I tug the sweatpants on and over my hips, my hands pausing over the hem of my nightshirt before I yank it over my head.

"Jesus," I hear Reuben mutter as salt air washes over my bare nipples. I smirk at my lap and tug his sweatshirt on, taking my sweet time.

Gentle hands roll the socks onto my feet. I close my eyes and savor his touch. All too soon, it's over, and he stands again, frowning at my feet.

"I don't have shoes for you."

I shrug, hopping out of the car. The stone of the parking lot is cold through my socks.

"That's okay."

He sweeps me up into his arms before the words are out of my mouth. I yelp, winding my arms around his neck, and Reuben looks way too smug as he locks up the car.

"Come on, princess. Let's get you some food."

I'm hungry for something, alright, but we won't find it in this diner.

* * *

If there were such a thing as a Lily Mountford theme park, this would be it. Sitting in a diner booth by the side of the coast road, sealed up against Reuben's side. His arm clamps around me, crushing me close, and I *love* it. I melt into him like gooey milk chocolate.

He orders for both of us in his gruff voice, picking my favorites without having to ask. And when the pancakes arrive, drizzled in syrup with crispy bacon stacked on top, he scoops up my fork and feeds me bites by hand.

I lick a glob of syrup off his thumb knuckle, holding his gaze.

A shudder ripples through his big body.

There's no need for this. I can feed myself, and there's no one in this diner who might recognize me. Yet here we are, slipping back into our games as easy as breathing.

I nip at his fingertip. Reuben growls.

"Behave yourself, princess."

"Or what?" I ask, my heart skittering. Whatever the consequences are, I already know I want them.

Reuben leans down, speaking into my hair. His beard brushes against the shell of my ear.

"Or I'll put you over my knee."

It's my turn to shiver, from the roots of my hair all the way down to my toes. I squeeze my thighs together inside his warm, fleecy sweatpants.

"I don't believe you." Reuben feeds me another forkful of pancake and I chew, raising my eyebrows.

"No?" He chuckles. "Then why are your cheeks so red?"

Damn it. I can never be *cool* with Reuben. Mature and sophisticated. Even on photo shoots for the burgeoning model career my father wanted for me, Reuben's eyes on me always made me feel like a gawky teenager.

I'm nineteen years old. An adult. So why do I want him babying me more than my next breath?

I swallow, reaching for my milky coffee with a frown. Being around him, so *close* to him, enveloped in his scent—it's twisting my insides into knots.

But I can't forget the way he pushed me away. The way he keeps knocking me back, the rejection battering my heart.

Suddenly, I don't want to play anymore. I clear my throat, ducking out from under his arm and sliding along in the booth. Not far—just enough to put some space between us. I avoid his eyes, plucking up the spare fork and feeding myself the rest of my breakfast.

A tense silence follows us back across the parking lot. Reuben is agitated, raking his hand through his dark hair. His huge boots echo on the stone, and I'm struck again just how big and bulky he is. How heavy he'd be on top of me.

I push the thought away. I have *some* pride, damn it.

I won't pine after a man who keeps turning me down. That's what I tell myself, anyway, as I pad across the parking lot in my socks. Reuben had tried to lift me again, but I waved him away, skirting out of reach. Now he scowls at the ground with every step I take, like I'm picking through broken glass and not walking over smooth concrete.

I head toward the back of the car, but Reuben grunts and opens the front passenger side. Fine. It makes no difference to me. I slide into the car seat, nodding in thanks.

He grunts again, all riled up, but he slams the door shut and storms around to the driver's side.

"Do you have to be so pissy?" I snap as he throws himself bodily into the seat. He glares at me, wrenching the door closed.

"Seat belt."

Ugh. I clip myself in and fold my arms, my hands drowned inside his sleeves.

The sweatshirt smells like him. I tuck my nose inside the collar and breathe, staring out the window. After a long moment, the engine growls to life, the vibration buzzing through the seat.

Still, we don't pull away. After a minute, I glance over.

Reuben watches me, his rough face troubled.

"I'm sorry, princess," he mutters at last. If I weren't constantly straining to hear his every movement, I might have missed it.

I shrug one shoulder.

"Me too," I rasp.

He nods, and we pull onto the road.

Reuben

I'm not going to manage this. I've made a huge fucking mistake.
Every time she bats those big green eyes at me, my willpower
fades a little more.

I'll never get her to the safety of my aunt's ranch untouched.

Not when Lily squirms so hot and needy under my gaze.
Not when she sighs and melts into me like there's no place
she'd rather be.

I'm not a fool. It's normal that Lily would be... curious. That
she would want to experiment. Explore.

But I'm not the man for her to do it with. If I got my hands
on her, I'd never let go. I'd own her, body and soul, demanding
every last part of her. I'd consume her, and be entirely hers in
turn.

Besides, it's not *me* she wants. I'm just the closest man, and
the only one she trusts. One day, now that she's out of her
father's grip, she'll meet a boy. Someone her age. And she'll
look at him the way she looks at me sometimes—like she'd die
and go to heaven for a single kiss.

I clench the steering wheel until it creaks.

I can't fucking think about this. It makes me want to tear this car apart, to rip the doors off with my bare hands.

"What are you thinking about?" Lily murmurs from the passenger seat.

"Karma," I clip out.

The agitation snaking through me only builds through the day. We stop off in a strange city and ditch the car, moving the few supplies I brought into a new ride. I drop a chunk of my savings on the new car without blinking.

It's worth it to keep Lily safe.

We go by new names out here. She picks the same last name as me, pretending to be my young wife just to torment me.

By the time late afternoon rolls around, as we drive along the endless coast road, the novelty has worn off. She's bored. She plucks at my sweater where it clings to my shoulder. Then scrambles around on the passenger seat and rests her feet in my lap.

Jesus. I breathe in hard through my nose and will my cock to stop swelling.

"Where are we going, again?"

"I told you. Somewhere safe."

She scoffs, and the sound makes my mouth twitch.

"Right, yeah. Because *that's* a helpful answer."

I flex my fingers on the steering wheel. Over the last three years, I've taken great care not to share too much about myself with Lily.

It's a self-preservation thing. When I leave her at the ranch, I'll already be leaving my heart with her. I can't leave the rest of my soul too.

There's nothing for it, though. She needs to know where

we're headed, and she'll find out all about me one way or another.

About my parents dying when I was a child. Being raised on my aunt's ranch. Leaving for the military, then spending every night I was at war vowing to one day come back to that ranch.

I'd been on my way there when I took the job for Lily's father. I'd just been honorably discharged, and the bodyguard gig was meant to be a temporary thing. A few weeks of work to make a quick buck before heading back to the ranch.

I took one look at Lily and rented an apartment. The ranch could wait.

Going there now, taking her with me… it's like something out of a dream. So I keep pinching myself as I tell her about it—the open fields and the stables full of horses.

My aunt's cooking. The flocks of chickens pecking around the courtyard. The way the sunset lights the whole ranch up gold.

Lily listens to it all, her expression rapt. And I can't help but take one hand off the wheel, massaging the arch of her foot. She moans, her eyelids fluttering closed, and now my hard-on is back with a vengeance.

I drop her foot, clearing my throat, and look back at the road. The ranch is a long way yet.

"My aunt will take good care of you." It's the only comfort I have for what's coming. "And I'll send you money. Enough to live well. Maybe even go to college."

Lily's gasp slices to my core.

"You're not staying with me?" Her voice hardens. "You're *leaving* me there? Like some orphaned puppy?"

"Lily…"

She snatches her feet off my lap. And turns around so far

in her seat, I can only see the back of her head. Her golden brown hair is still snarled and messy from our... altercation in the night.

I grit my teeth, pressing harder on the accelerator. The sooner I'm far away from her, the better.

* * *

I drive until the light fades and only headlights swoop through the darkness. Only then do I pull off the highway, our car rumbling to a stop in a motel parking lot.

"Wait here."

Lily doesn't reply. I debate carrying her inside under my arm, but decide it's better not to draw attention.

Besides, where would she run? And she's clearly come to the same conclusion, because when I step back outside the reception with a key clutched in one hand, she's still glowering at me from the passenger seat.

"Let's go."

She gets out without a word. She even waits quietly while I grab our things from the trunk. But when I reach for her, to carry her over the dark path to our motel room, she steps out of reach.

God damn it.

The room is clean. Sparse but cozy enough. A light bulb dangles from the ceiling, and a boxy old television hunkers against the far wall. There's a small refrigerator, a shadowed doorway that must be the bathroom, and the bed.

The only bed.

I hold my palms up as Lily turns to me, eyebrows raised.

"This was the only room left. I'll sleep on the floor."

She sighs, shoulders slumping.

"Of course you will," she mutters, then marches to the bathroom. The door closes behind her with a snap. After a short pause, the shower comes on, the drumming of water drifting through the wall.

I palm my hardening cock through my jeans, trying not to let my mind wander to her hot, flushed skin—to the streams of water pouring down her curves.

"Fuck," I mutter, locking our door behind us and kicking off my boots. It's fucked up, but this is my only hope for relief. While she's safely locked behind that door, far away from my twisted thoughts.

My cock strains against my jeans as I tug my zipper down. One, two strokes, and my head is already swimming. She's been *right fucking there* all day, with her little sighs and her goddamn scent—

"Reuben?"

Her shocked voice echoes from the doorway. She leans against the door frame, her wide eyes fixed on my cock.

I'm a monster. I can't help it. I snarl and pump my fist again.

"Go back inside. Lock the door, princess."

She licks her lips, hypnotized. "I forgot a towel," she murmurs, like she didn't even hear me.

"Lily," I grind out, jerking my cock harder. With her eyes on me, everything is dialed up brighter. The feel of my rough grip, the brush of my clothes against my skin, the trembling breaths sucking in and out of her sweet chest. *"Lily.* You don't want to see this."

I layer all the command I can manage into my voice, and

it jerks her from her daze. She looks up at me, her cheeks flushed.

"Yes I do," she whispers, and my knees nearly buckle. I stroke myself harder, faster, as she crosses the room, the rasp of my breath loud and hungry.

"Don't," I grit as she reaches her fingertips toward my cock. She pauses, her hand hovering, and she looks up at me with those wide eyes.

"No?" Her lips turn down, her face so fucking sad, and she starts to pull her hand back. Starts to turn away. She won't push me; I have to own it. If I want Lily's hands on me, I have to admit it out loud.

"Fuck. Yes. Lily, touch me."

She spins back to face me, lit up like I've bought her a damn pony. Like I've showered her with diamonds, not offered her my thick cock. She sinks to her knees, and fuck, I didn't mean she should do *that*, but when her lips fasten around the head, I let out a hollow groan. I'm the worst kind of man, but my hips snap forward and my hands burrow in her hair.

Lily moans around my cock, her tongue swirling over the sensitive skin, and I hiss.

"You like that, do you princess? You like a man fucking your sweet mouth?"

She pulls off me with a wet pop, jerking the base of my shaft with her small fist.

"Not *a man*, Reuben. *You.*"

I snarl, pushing back between those plump lips. Her eyelids flutter as her cheeks hollow, sucking all the blood to my head. My balls are heavy, ready to burst, and they draw up tight to my body. Her hands drift down her body, tweaking at her nipples through my sweatshirt, and I groan, pushing deeper into her throat.

It's wrong. It's so fucking wrong—rough and primal and everything Lily is not. But she *loves* it—my princess moans on her knees, bobbing her head in time with my thrusts. A hint of teeth scrapes over my shaft, and I see stars.

"Lily." I tug her hair. "Lily, fuck. I'm going to come."

Her eyes blink open again and she holds my eyes as she takes my cock as deep as it will go. I curse, filthy praise falling from my lips as I empty into her mouth, feeding her spurt after spurt.

She takes it all.

She hums and swallows it all down, like it's more syrup from the diner and not my salty cum. Lily trails her palms over her body as she sucks me, squeezing her own waist and twisting her nipples, writhing on her poor knees, and she might as well give me a road map.

Where she wants to be touched. And how.

The second that last spurt of my release hits her tongue, I tuck my cock back into my jeans and scoop her up. I carry her over to the bed, tossing her onto the mattress like a rag doll. I know how much she loves that.

Sure enough, a shocked laugh bursts out of her, then she's gazing up at me as her legs drop open.

Yes, a voice roars in my head. Triumph swells my chest; makes me want to beat my fists against my sternum.

That is what I want to see every day for the rest of my life.

I can't, though. Even this moment of weakness aside, Lily deserves better.

Still, I crawl onto the bed after her, growling as she moans and reaches for me.

If I'm going to hell, I'm doing it properly. With the sound of

Lily's orgasm ringing in my ears.

Lily

~~~

If my knees weren't throbbing from kneeling on the cold, hard floor, if my jaw weren't aching and sore, I'd probably think this was a dream again.

I've pictured this so many times. The glint in Reuben's eyes as he crawls up my body, his bulk dwarfing me against the mattress. The soft brush of his beard under my fingertips; the nip of his teeth against the pad of my thumb.

I've wanted this for *so long*. My heart shudders inside my chest, primed to shatter.

"Please," I breathe as a shadow passes over Reuben's face. He rakes his gaze over me, from my wild hair to my socked feet, and his mouth twists in dismay. I grab fistfuls of his black sweater, tugging at him like I could shake the doubt clean out of him. "Please, Reuben. I want this. I want it so bad."

He opens his mouth like he's going to argue, so I lunge up and capture his mouth with my own. The taste of him is still in my mouth, salty and delicious, and Reuben groans as my tongue slides between his lips.

"Stop if you want to," I murmur between kisses. My head is light and spinning. "But only if you really don't want this. Don't choose for me, Reuben. I can't bear it."

His broad shoulders vibrate with tension under my palms. He scowls down at me, eyes tortured as I flop back against the bed. And when he snaps, tearing his sweatpants down my legs in one rough motion, I grin and punch the air.

"Come on." I hook my legs around his waist, rubbing the damp spot on my panties against his jeans. "Take me. Take me rough. I can handle it."

I'm babbling, only half aware of what I'm saying. I'm talking a big game, but *no one* has been inside me before.

I have no idea what I can take. Only that if Reuben's the one giving it to me, I need it more than air.

But he's already shaking his head, hooking his hands under my knees to peel me off. I prop myself on my elbows, panic and hurt warring in my chest, but Reuben places one big hand on each of my bare thighs and presses me wide open. He shuffles down the bed, settling his huge frame between my legs.

Yes.

I drop back against the mattress, squirming and panting fast. He smooths a thumb over my panties, his calluses catching on the lace, and my pussy clenches down on nothing.

"I knew you'd be a needy little thing." He's muttering, half to himself, and I bite my lip. I can't deny it—I'm so desperate for him, I can't lie still.

"Is that bad?" I gasp at the ceiling. A flush creeps over my cheeks.

What if I'm doing this all wrong?

"*No.*" That word shudders through me, almost angry in its denial. I sink deeper into the mattress, relieved.

When his thumbs hook in my panties, I hold my breath. I lift my hips to help him pull them down my thighs. He goes slow, so slow, and if he doesn't touch me right this second my heart is going to slam straight out my chest—

Reuben licks a broad stripe up my pussy, covering every inch of me in one go. I squeal, twisting and writhing on the bed, but he holds me down as he rubs his face in my core.

"Oh, no you don't." He rubs my clit with his nose, and I whimper. His beard tickles the soft skin of my inner thighs. "We've come this far, princess. You're not wriggling away until you've come on my tongue."

Every drum beat of my heart is triumphant—*yes, yes, yes*—and I feel myself grow slicker with each passing second. Reuben growls his approval, licking and sucking on me, grinding his whole face into my private parts.

I scrabble at the bed covers, twisting them in my grip, before my hands flutter to Reuben's shoulders. He's so freaking big compared to me, his collarbone like scaffolding under my palms, and for a second I remember the size of his cock.

"That's it," he mutters as I groan, my pussy clenching. "Show me how bad you want it."

"So bad," I gasp. "Please, Reuben. Give it to me."

A shudder ripples through him, but he shakes his head.

"Not today," is all he says, and I open my mouth to argue but he swirls his tongue around my clit and *sucks.* My legs lock up, my muscles shaking, and hot, aching pleasure rolls through me in waves. I might be screaming, I don't know, but when I finally come back to myself, I'm crashed out on the mattress with my ears ringing.

My harsh breaths slow.

I reach out a languid arm.

And brush against a chest that's vibrating with tension.

I prop myself up on my elbows as Reuben tugs the sweatpants back up my legs. He double knots the tie at my waist with a furious scowl as I whisper his name.

He scrubs a hand over his beard, his face gaunt with regret. I try to catch his eye, but his gaze is fixed on the mattress beside me.

Then he pushes off the bed and storms out of the motel room, slamming the door behind him.

* * *

Okay. Okay.

This isn't how I'd pictured this part.

I know Reuben is gruff. I love that about him. So I figured he probably wasn't a cuddler.

But whenever I dreamed of this moment, fantasizing in the shower or in my dark bedroom at night, I always thought that he'd at least *stay*. That he'd tuck my hair behind my ear. Murmur nice things to me. Or if not nice things, deliciously naughty ones.

I force myself to sit up, my limbs like jelly, and blink at the closed motel door. The room is silent except for the wind rattling the window, and the shower still drumming in the en suite. I wrap my arms around my legs, tucking my knees to my chest, and stare at the scratched wood, willing him to come back.

Maybe he forgot something in the car.

Maybe he needs to make a call.

Maybe...

He doesn't want me.

All this time, I thought we were playing the same game. A twisted game, maybe, but a secret, special game between *us*.

Where we both knew the rules. Where we both knew what was coming at the end: us together, never letting go.

Maybe I didn't know the rules at all.

After all, that's not the plan, is it? Reuben's version of this ends with me left alone at the ranch, as he drives off into the distance. To continue his life without me in it. Maybe to meet someone. Start a family.

A pit yawns open wide in my chest and I choke back a sob. I keep staring at that motel door, but it stays shut. Silent and ruthless. My breath starts to wheeze in and out of my lungs. Suddenly I can't bear to have Reuben's clothes on me anymore, to be wrapped in his scent. I tear them off, fast and clumsy enough to rip the seams, flinging them at the ugly wallpaper.

He warned me, alright.

Plenty of times, he tried to tell me. He might want my pussy, might want my mouth wrapped around his cock, but when we're done with all that he doesn't want *me*. All those times, I thought he was being noble. Trying to protect me because he's older, rougher, *wild*.

I dig the heels of my palms into my eyes, my toes curling on the scratchy carpet.

Well, I won't cry for him anymore. Even as my chest aches so bad it might burst, I refuse to shed another tear.

I'm strong, even if he doesn't see it. I can make my own way.

And I plan to. Away from *him*.

Reuben

The sky is inky black by the time I go back inside. Bats flap overhead, deeper shadows in the night.

I've done my thinking. Got my head on straight, with the fresh ocean breeze slapping my flushed cheeks.

Lily is *mine*.

I may be too old for her. Too scared, too big, too brash. But I don't care anymore.

I've touched her, and I'm never letting her go.

It's ridiculous, but I haven't been this nervous since I was a gawky teenager trying to figure out girls for the first time. What if I've misread this?

What if she just wanted to act out a fantasy, to defy her father one last time by sleeping with the help?

I have to ask. I have to know for sure, either way. Because if there's any chance Lily feels like I do...

I can't risk not knowing. I'm going to war one last time.

The motel room is weirdly quiet when I push the door open. I scan it quickly, frowning at what I find. The clothes I lent her are bunched and twisted, strewn all over the carpet. The bed covers are rucked up from our bodies, and just that sight alone is enough to send my blood pumping south.

My cock hardens, and I palm the front of my jeans.

Not this time. I can't get distracted. The stakes are too high.

The bathroom door creaks open and Lily steps through, dressed in her nightshirt again. Her hair is damp from the shower, braided over one shoulder, and her skin is pink from scrubbing.

My mouth waters, but something stops me from lunging for her. The cold, distant smile she gives me.

"You said you'd sleep on the floor, right?"

I nod, my gut clenching. My pulse thuds so loud, I can hear it in my ears. Lily trips past, an ice princess dismissing her subject.

Fuck.

Fuck.

It's everything I feared. I'm good for a roll in bed, but that's all I am to her. A hard, warm body, and a way to piss off her father.

I shut myself in the bathroom for a moment. I need time to catch my breath, to stare into my own dead eyes in the mirror. I look lost. Broken from the inside out.

It was just another game, then. Right. Fine.

At least I know for sure.

I splash my face with cold water. Scrub my teeth, then say fuck it and take an icy shower.

When I emerge from the bathroom, the lights are off and Lily lies alone in the bed. She's turned away, the covers tugging up over her slender shoulders, her breaths coming slow and even.

I don't bother searching for a pillow or blanket. I lie on the floor beside the bed in a daze. Somewhere in the room, a clock ticks, each passing second digging into my brain.

I won't push her. Won't chase her. I'm not a monster.

Not in that way, anyway.

Lily

There's something wrong with Reuben. I shouldn't care—I don't want to care—but three years of unrequited love for this man can't just be wiped out in one night. He packs up the car in silence, his jaw clenched tight, and he won't meet my eye.

The regret is killing him. He's always been so ashamed of his attraction for me. And I pushed him to this—teased and taunted him until the last thread of his control snapped.

It wasn't a game to me. I wanted him forever. But I still can't deny that this is my fault.

I've broken a good man. So when he opens the passenger door for me, I pause and rest my hand on his shoulder.

"I'm sorry, Reuben."

He shrugs me off like I've burned him.

"Get in," is all he says.

Now *that* is familiar. He's always been blunt. Always loved to boss me around. And I've loved it too, an ache throbbing in my core whenever he uses that commanding tone on me.

That was before. *Now* it pisses me off. I toss my hair and use my best icy tone.

"Don't speak to me like that."

He laughs, hollow.

"It never bothered you before."

I jab him in the chest.

"You'd never made me come then *ditched* me before."

He blinks, expression shocked, but I've said too much. I couldn't keep the raw hurt from bleeding into my words. I duck inside the car, sliding onto the seat and tugging the door closed behind me. I've just clipped my seat belt in when the door wrenches open again.

"Say that again." Reuben fills the doorway, a vicious glint in his eye. The ocean breeze washes in behind him, tinting the air with salt and brine. Behind him, the motel parking lot is washed blue by the cold light of dawn.

I jut out my chin.

"No."

I don't take orders anymore. And I won't bare all my hurt for him to get twisted up over. It's *mine*, and I'll keep it to myself, thank you very much.

He takes my chin in his big fingers and forces me to look at him. Well, too bad he can't grip my eyeballs. I scowl up at the car ceiling.

"*Lily.*"

"What?" I grind out between my teeth.

"Say it again," he begs.

Something about the desperate way he speaks sends the air rushing out of my lungs. A silly, traitorous hope tickles at my chest, but I push it away. I force my words out flat and hollow.

"I said you hadn't made me come and then ditched me before." I meet his gaze, my eyes blazing. "Are you happy?"

"Yes," he snaps, then grips the back of my head. He tugs my mouth against his, kissing me like an addict getting his fix, groaning loud and long. I stay frozen for a moment until he grunts, touching my waist, tugging my hair, then my control snaps. I melt against him, sliding my tongue against his. My whole body flushes hot, my heart somersaulting in my chest, and that premature swoop of triumph is what shatters the moment.

"Wait." I push him away when my brain comes back online. He moves back, but only by an inch. His chest heaves like he's been running a marathon, and that gives me courage. "Is this another game? I don't want to play anymore, Reuben."

"It's never been a game," he growls, resting his forehead against mine. I suck in a shaky breath, touching his beard with shy fingertips.

"You really want me?" I whisper.

"*Lily.*" He groans. "More than anything. It might make me a monster—"

"Shut up. No, it doesn't."

"—but I can't keep away any longer. Now that I've tasted you…" His chest heaves up and down. I watch it, hypnotized. "I won't let you go."

My eyes drop shut. How long have I yearned for those words? He plucks at my nightshirt, concerned, but a smile curves my lips.

"Princess," he murmurs, and I unclip my belt and wriggle around in the seat. I turn to face him, wedging my legs on either side of his hips.

I raise my chin and hold his gaze. Quirk my eyebrow in challenge.

"Prove it." I roll my body toward him.

Reuben groans, plunging his hands under my nightshirt to find I'm not wearing any panties. I'm bare to the ocean breeze, wet and pink for anyone to see, but there's no one out here but us.

"Jesus Christ," he mutters, his thumb flicking over my clit.

Well. There's us, and whoever happens to glance through their motel window. I don't care. If anything, the thought makes me more eager.

I want everyone to see Reuben claiming me. To see me claim him in turn. So when he tries to climb inside the car with me, then shakes his head and mutters, "Fuck this," I'm thrilled that he scoops me up and brings me out into the air. He presses me against the side of the car, the whole vehicle rocking as he thrusts against my bare pussy, his forehead resting on my shoulder.

"This is wrong," he murmurs into my ear. "A good man wouldn't take you out here. Wouldn't fuck you for the first time in broad daylight, up against a car."

"Then I don't want a good man." I nip at his throat, reaching between us to pop open the button on his jeans. "I want *this*." I wrap my hand around his cock.

He's already so hard it looks painful, rigid as steel in my palm. Reuben lets me rub the head against my slick pussy, humming and teasing.

He glances at the nearest window.

"Someone might see."

"*Good*," I hiss. "Let's give them a show."

He snarls, snapping his hips up and burying the first three inches inside me. It's a tight fit, he's so freaking huge, and the stretch and burn of him steals my breath.

"Keep going," I gasp when he stills. He grunts and shoves

forward another few inches, my channel twitching around his cock.

"Does it hurt?" he mutters in my ear. I giggle, lightheaded.

"*Yes.* It's perfect."

That's what breaks him. What makes him groan and thrust forward, filling me to the hilt. My ankles hook behind his back, and his grip on my thighs is tight enough to bruise. It's sinful, so perfect, and when his palm cracks against my ass cheek, I jerk up in his arms, surprised.

"Yeah, I knew you'd like that. Always begging to be put over my knee."

I gasp and nod, writhing on the hard length of him. He pulses in and out, spanking my ass and growling filthy things in my ear. Things that make me clench and ripple around him.

The sting of his invasion is fading now, and the hot slide of him in and out makes my toes curl in my socks. It's heady, all-consuming. Taking me over from the inside out.

"Fuck," Reuben grits out. "Look at you. A needy virgin princess. You can't get enough, can you?" He shoves deeper, hips snapping up.

I shake my head, teeth chattering. Too far gone for words. Reuben thrusts harder and faster and I see stars. Every push of his hips brushes over my clit, and the pleasure is building in my core, hot and achy. It winds tighter and tighter, coiling up my insides, and when Reuben grabs a fistful of my hair and *yanks*, I come apart with a cry.

He keeps thrusting through it all, murmuring filthy praise in my ear, telling me how good I feel on his cock. How I was made to take him, to let him inside. Then he follows me over the edge, slamming deep into my pussy and emptying everything into my core.

104

I wrap my arms around his neck, clinging on for dear life. The groan he lets out sounds like it was dredged up from his soul.

We slump against the car together, breathing hard.

"This is it, princess." He speaks after long minutes standing together, sticky and cooling but pressed tight against the metal. "No running. No changing your mind. I warned you, and now you're *mine*."

I'm already nodding. That's what I've always wanted. What I've been teasing and begging him for.

"You're mine too," I tell him, just to be a brat. "Don't you dare look at another woman. Not for the rest of your life."

He tosses his head back and laughs, the sound echoing through the parking lot.

"What other women? Since the day I met you, I've only seen you."

My grin makes my cheeks ache.

We bundle back into the car, but it's different this time. Reuben's always touching me, glancing over. He can't keep his hands off me. I bite my lip, then swivel in my seat again and rest my feet in his lap. He hums in approval.

I'm excited for the ranch, yes, but most of all I wish this drive could last forever.

It's perfect. *He's* perfect. And the tickle in my belly is already starting up again.

Reuben snorts. "Don't look at me like that. I'll drive the car off the road."

"Sorry," I whisper, my smirk telling him I'm not sorry at all.

I'll never be sorry for any of it.

Reuben

~~~~~~~~~~~~~~~~~~~~~~~~~~~~~~

Three months later

The last time I saw Lily in a wedding dress, she was crying. Her beautiful face was pale and shocked, and she kept throwing desperate glances at me as her father's tailor measured her, tucking up her hem.

That day took every ounce of my self control. Already, a dozen plans whirred through my head—a dozen ways to get Lily out of this arranged marriage.

Today tests my self control just as badly, but for an entirely different reason.

Lily's cheeks are flushed as she stands in her gown on the grassy cliff above the sea. Her dress is simple and elegant, the white silk skimming her frame like a Grecian goddess. Her golden brown hair is pinned up in an elaborate updo—one with twisting braids and dotted pearls that her twin sister Nora did for her this morning.

Nora is here now, clutching the Fox's hand and beaming as

they wait for the priest to say the words. Beside them, my aunt and cousins watch too, glowing with pride. They loved Lily the moment she stepped foot on the ranch.

One day soon, she'll have a ranch all her own. Her own stables and horses; her own cozy farmhouse. I already put down the deposit. I'm surprising her with her new home after our honeymoon in Italy.

Lily glances around, nervous, but Mountford isn't here. He wouldn't dare show his face, not after my little visit two months ago.

I just wanted to say hi. Catch up. Inform him that Lily was mine now, and that she never wanted to see him again. Oh, and that if he gave us any trouble, I'd carve out his heart and leave it still beating on his desk

I think he believed me. The knife I was picking my nails with didn't hurt.

I wrap an arm around my bride, speaking with my lips against her temple.

"He's not coming, princess. You never have to fear him again."

She shivers, but this time it's not from fear. When she smiles up at me, her pupils are dilated.

Fuck.

I already took her twice this morning, but the second I leave the place between her thighs, I want to go back again. Nowhere else feels like home to me. I *need* her, need to feel her hot and wet around me, sighing in my ear.

She's my ruin.

My salvation.

I press a kiss to her hair, my throat tight.

The ceremony is short. Simple. We don't need to convince

anyone else of our love; we're just here to make it official. And so that I can selfishly see my bride in a wedding gown, and tuck that image away in my mind forever.

"I do," Lily breathes, her eyes wide as she gazes up at me. Her lips are slightly parted, and I want to slide my thumb into her mouth. She bites her lip like she knows exactly what I'm thinking, her faint giggle snatched away by the breeze.

"I do," I grit out.

This is it. The beginning of everything. A life together—one without games.

Well. All but the fun kind, anyway. And my princess loves to play her games, loves to tease me and wind me around her finger. I'm helpless to resist, a puppet on her strings, but I love it too.

Especially when her goal is always my mouth on her pussy; her hands on my cock; my length shoved deep inside her. This morning, I spanked her ass so hard I left a pink hand print. She came and showed me, grinning and proud.

Fuck. What did a big, grumpy beast like me do to deserve a prize like her?

I was her bodyguard. Now I'm her husband. My heart throbs in my chest as we seal it with a kiss.

This is the beginning, and I dip her back. Kiss her right, until she's swooning in my arms and our small audience is whooping.

The sun dips below the horizon, painting the sky above the ocean pink.

The first day of the rest of our lives.

III

Fake Model

Coral

꧁ꕥ꧂

I'm icing a vanilla cupcake in our kitchen when my sister bursts through the front door. She's a whirlwind of color, her sapphire blue top slipping down one arm, and our signature red hair escaping from the messy bun on the crown of her head.

"Coral! Oh my god. I'm so glad you're here. You won't believe it. *Coral.*"

Where else would I be? I'm not larger than life like my twin sister. She goes to parties and gallery openings and red carpet events. She meets with fashion designers and struts down catwalks.

Me? I clean a billionaire's house, and I hang out here. In our sunlit kitchen. The afternoon light filters through our big windows, washing over my potted herbs nestled on the windowsill. The wall tiles are white and sparkling clean, and the room smells like warm cupcakes.

Seriously. Why would I leave?

"What is it?" I murmur as Billie charges toward me, weaving

between our sofa and coffee table with a big grin. She doesn't slow down when she reaches me, barreling into me and throwing her arms around my neck.

"I booked it!" she squeals into my hair, squeezing me and rocking me from side to side. I wince and hug her back, happy for her but still kind of sorry for the smeared cupcake wilting on the countertop.

"Oh." Billie pulls back, her smile fading into a look of dismay. She looks so sorry when she glances from the cupcake back to me that it's impossible to be mad. I snort, nudging the warm cake toward her.

"You can have the messy one."

She bites her lip, eyes shining again.

"I don't know if I should. I've waited so long for this, Coral. I can't afford to overeat now."

I nod and shrug, trying not to feel hurt. This is the only physical difference between Billie and I—she keeps her body svelte and slender for her modeling career, always hitting the gym and going on runs and drinking green smoothies, while I...

Well, my hobby is cake decorating.

And hey, I like yoga. Once in a while.

"Save it for me." She squeezes my arm. "The shoot is in two days. I'll eat it after that, and I swear, I will savor every bite."

"You don't have to do that." I duck my head, embarrassed, but I can't help my faint smile. Billie is my biggest fan, and I'm hers. That's how we've always been. We left home together, rented this apartment together, and we've had each other's backs the whole time.

Billie's the one who keeps nudging me to put my cake designs online. To try and start a following, and maybe even my own business.

She says I can do it. That I'm more than talented enough. That I'm wasted cleaning a rich man's house.

I'm not so sure. The thought of people *looking* at me, at my designs, even through a computer...

I shiver, my skin flashing cold.

Billie hops up onto the kitchen counter, her heels bouncing off the cupboards as she chatters away. Telling me all about the man she's so excited to work with—the photographer Archer Westbrook. He's famously moody and impenetrable, prowling around shoots, but he's the best. The man with the unstoppable talent.

The model-maker.

The man who can set your career alight, who holds people's hopes and dreams in the palm of his hand. Billie is starry-eyed, beaming at the ceiling.

I bite the inside of my cheek as I listen, icing the rest of the cupcakes carefully. What must it be like, working with a man like that? Going toe to toe with a titan? She's shown me a photo of him before, and the man looks like the reincarnation of Thor. Only grumpier.

Billie is far braver than me. I'd run and hide under the table.

"Oh, Coral." Billie leans closer, sighing from her seat on the counter. "Seashells? They're so pretty."

I shoot her a grin from behind my hair. I've been working on this design for a while, and it's finally perfect. Each cupcake is a different seashell, with cream icing tinted with pale pink and blue. There's even an oyster, opening wide to show off its pearl.

"You should take a photo," Billie says suddenly. "Or I could take one for you. We could put it online, start some social media accounts for your business."

I shrug, grabbing the mixing bowl and crossing to the sink.

Billie doesn't push me. She lets me run away, hiding in the drumming of the running water and the big stack of washing up. But after a long moment, I hear the smack of her sandals against the kitchen tiles, then the *click* of her camera.

I don't say anything. I'm too tongue-tied, my throat tight with nerves.

Another time. I'll do it another time.

When I'm feeling brave.

***

My phone chirps the next day as I'm straining to dust my boss's bookcase. The tech mogul Eli Koven is a big reader, with bookcases lining the walls of most rooms in his mansion. But *this* one has his collection of first edition hardbacks, the leather spines lined up neat and perfect.

They're priceless. Worth more than everything Billie and I own combined.

And they're freaking dust magnets.

My phone chirps again as I stretch to reach the top shelf. There's a stepladder I could use, but the cupboard is all the way down the hall, and if I could just *reach*—

Chirp.

I curse under my breath and rock back on my heels. With a quick glance to check for cameras or prying eyes, I dig my phone out of my maid's tunic.

No one texts me except Billie, and she knows I'm at work. She wouldn't interrupt unless it was important.

My heart thumps faster as I read her text, scanning it over and over until my vision blurs.

Billie: At the hospital. Had an accident. Can you come get me after your shift?

I swallow, mouth dry. My boss Mr. Koven is strict. Exacting. He doesn't employ slackers—or certainly not for long. And while maybe I could try and talk to him, ask if I could leave early...

My throat clamps tight at the thought. My palms grow damp with sweat.

Crap. *Crap.* I can't let my sister down like this. But there's no way on this planet that I could talk to Mr. Koven. Already, I can feel the stutter tripping up my tongue.

My cheeks flush crimson. No. Not an option.

I glance at the clock on the wall of Mr. Koven's study. 2:03pm. There are two hours left of my shift.

"Screw it," I mutter, shooting Billie a quick reply and stuffing the phone back in my pocket. I tiptoe out into the hallway, duster clutched in one hand.

Mr. Koven's housekeeper smiles at me distantly as I speed-walk past, nodding and dropping my eyes. She doesn't say anything, even when I stuff the duster back into the cupboard and hurry down the main staircase, my shoes thudding on the thick carpet.

That's the good part of being invisible.

No one sees me leave.

* * *

My poor sister looks rumpled and exhausted in her hospital bed. She's fully dressed in denim shorts and a light sweater, her body stretched out on top of the covers with her bag perched ready by her feet. But even she can't disguise her winces of pain as she tries to sit up, her snarled red hair tumbling over one shoulder.

"What happened?"

I rush to her side, checking her over for cuts and bruises. There's a graze on her cheekbone, but that's mostly it. She seems almost normal except for one thing: the plaster cast wrapped around one forearm. It's tucked against her chest with a sling, and the fingers curling out of the plaster are battered and bruised.

"Freaking cyclist," she grumbles, hissing in a sharp breath as she straightens up. "He came barreling out of nowhere, right down the sidewalk. Coral..." Billie stops and swallows. I know her heart's breaking when her chin wobbles. She whispers her next words. "I can't do the shoot. My career is over."

"That's not true." I help her off the bed, my mind spinning. That can't be right. Can it? "It's just one canceled booking. It must happen to everyone sometimes."

Billie snorts, but there's no humor in it.

"No one cancels on Archer Westbrook."

I huff, annoyed on her behalf. Who does this Archer Westbrook think he is, the king of England? Of course people need to cancel sometimes. I tell her so, too, wrapping my arm around her waist and supporting her stiff steps to the hospital doorway.

"You just don't get it," Billie mutters, blowing a strand of hair out of her face. "This was *it*, Coral. My shot. And I already blew it."

116

I open my mouth to tell her she's wrong, that there will be other opportunities, but I swallow the words back when a doctor strides over. His footsteps are loud in the hallway, his white coat billowing behind him, and his confidence is like a hand wrapped around my throat.

He begins to speak to me, clipping out instructions about painkillers and washing my arm. He thinks I'm Billie. It's only when he looks down and sees the cast on her arm instead that he blinks and gives himself a little shake. Apologizes and talks to the right sister.

She answers his questions, murmuring careful replies, but I'm not fooled. I know Billie.

I can see the wheels turning in her head.

The second he's gone, she spins to face me, eyes bright and crafty. I hold up my palms, back up against the hospital wall. The corridor is lined with cork-boards and peeling posters about anatomy, and the frayed corner of one tickles in my hair.

"No," I beg. "I can't do it. Billie, don't ask me."

"It's just one shoot," she pleads. "A few hours, tops. It could save my whole *career*."

I wave an arm up and down my body. Over my curves, so much rounder than hers, and my maid's tunic.

I could not be less of a model if I tried.

"No one is going to buy it, Billie! What if I can't fit into the clothes? And what if they need me to *sp-speak*—"

"You can do it." She smooths a palm down my arm. "You're beautiful, Coral. Clothes need to be adjusted all the time at shoots. And you don't have to speak. Just say you've lost your voice. Take a note."

I chew on my lip, staring at the floor. At my sensible maid's shoes, next to my sister's pretty sandals.

Could I really do this?

Some part of me has always wondered… if things were different… if *I* were different…

Would I be as magical as Billie?

A thought slams into my brain, crushing those tenuous hopes. I sigh, shoulders slumping.

"I can't, Billie. I have to work tomorrow. I already skipped out early today."

It's not like I can afford to lose this job. Billie's shoots bring in a lot of money when they happen, but they're not steady. We can't rely on them to pay our bills each month.

"I'll cover for you," she says at once. "I'll do your shift. If anyone asks, I'll say you sprained your wrist at work." She winks. "Then if they give you a hard time, you can sue."

She's joking, but I still squirm. I hate lying. And I *like* my job, mostly. It's quiet. Calming. And the views from the mansion windows are so pretty.

"I don't know…"

She begs me from the depths of her soul. *"Please."*

I've never been able to refuse my twin sister. And there's a small, secret part of me that's curious. That wants to try being Billie for a day.

That wants to be brave.

"Okay." I screw my eyes shut tight. "Okay. I'll try. But don't blame me if we get caught."

Billie whoops, catching me up in a one-armed hug, then hisses with pain. Her mood isn't dimmed for long, though. She's soon beaming at me again, eyes wide and grateful.

I trail her out to the parking lot, fiddling with my car keys, my heart sinking down to my shoes.

I hate people looking at me. I hate speaking in public.

And I *hate* bossy men who shout at me. What if this Archer Westbrook sees through our lie and lays into me in front of everyone? What if—what if he makes me cry?

I've always been such a baby. So quick to crumble in scary situations.

Oh god.

What the hell have I done?

Archer

❦

It's a dawn shoot on the beach, which means two things: sand fucking *everywhere*, and bucket loads of coffee. So much black coffee that energy crackles through my veins, and my vision sharpens as I glare through my camera lens.

Everyone else stifles yawns as they set up the equipment. The dress rails bristling with garment bags; the makeshift shelters for the model to change out of the wind. There are small tables set out with huge silver boilers of coffee, and covered baskets of muffins and fruit.

Across the long stretch of pale sand, clear blue waves froth and break on the beach. They're lazy too, the tide sighing and rolling over in its sleep.

Seabirds wheel overhead, screaming at the wisps of cloud. Shells dot the sand, either whole or in sharp white fragments.

It will do.

I turn to the dress rails, barking for one of my assistants to open the first garment bags. I want to see the material in the morning light, want to see how it reacts to the cold sun. I chew on the inside of my cheek, fiddling with my camera as I swap out lenses and check my memory cards.

"We'll start with the bridal gowns. Work backward through the styles and end on the lingerie." There's a squeak behind me, and I twitch my head to look, but my assistant comes and mutters in my ear.

"There's a problem."

Fuck. Already? There's no such thing as a perfect shoot, but we haven't even started. How have we gone wrong so fast?

I roll my head on my neck, annoyed. It's *my* name on the line, here. I'm at the top of this pyramid, which means if this shoot is a bust, I'm to blame.

I don't like fuck-ups. I don't make mistakes. So when I nod at Gavin to keep talking, I'm already grinding my teeth.

He lowers his voice, eyes darting away. He's uncomfortable.

"The model... she's bigger than the measurements we have on file. We need to take out the gowns."

I huff out a breath, pinching the bridge of my nose. I keep the best seamstresses in the business on standby for this exact reason, but it still pisses me the hell off. This model, this *Billie Blue Walsh*—she's supposed to be the best. I *only* work with the best.

And this? This is a rookie error. What kind of model doesn't update her measurements?

"Big breakfast?" I snarl, turning on my heel and pinning the girl with a glare. She's waiting a few feet back by the garment rail, wrapped in a robe with her arms clamped around her waist. She starts, her blue eyes widening, and a flush creeps over her cheeks. She tries to speak, her mouth opening and closing a few times, before she gives up and shakes her head, staring at her bare toes buried in the sand.

Shit. I've always been a grade A asshole, but a sliver of guilt squirms through my gut.

I tamp it down. I'm not here to make everyone feel good about themselves. This isn't an after school special; we're here to work.

Even if the sight of her creamy skin and red hair makes my chest seize.

I turn back to my camera, flipping through the settings, a new eagerness urging me on. For months now, I've been feeling... flat. Uninspired. I've been going through the motions, winning awards and making the front page of fashion magazines, but there's been no joy in it. No passion.

One glance at Billie Blue Walsh, and suddenly the love for my art comes rushing back. I want to capture the soulful depth to her eyes; want to pick out the copper highlights in her auburn curls.

A stuttered breath makes me turn around, dread freezing my veins.

She's dressed in the first gown, arms held out at her sides, two seamstresses altering it to fit. And she's staring off in a daze, a single tear rolling down her cheek.

Fuck.

Fuck.

What have I done?

One careless, throwaway question, borne out of impatience, and I made her *cry*.

I want to smash my camera over the rocks that line the edge of the beach. I want to walk into the goddamn sea. But I can't, because I need to make this right. I need to wipe that look of glazed horror off her face.

I need to show Billie Blue Walsh that she's the most beautiful creature I've ever seen.

***

It's odd. I picked the model for this shoot myself, flicking through hundreds of head shots and profiles. And while I thought Billie Blue had potential, had good cheekbones and striking eyes, her photos didn't *move* me.

Not like this.

Seeing her in person... I have a heart attack every time I glance over.

Gavin notices her crying too, and he's better at this than me. He takes her a coffee and a muffin from the basket. She waves the muffin off, a queasy look on her face, and I want to howl at the sky.

I don't know what I hate more—the fact that I've scared her off eating, or that *Gavin* is the man offering her comfort. I stride over without thinking, needing to break the two of them up.

"Are we ready?" I grit out, eying the two seamstresses. They glance up at me, mouths full of pins, and nod. I look down at Billie Blue, raising my eyebrows. She cringes under my gaze, but nods too.

I vow here and now that she won't be scared of me for long. That by the end of today, she'll look to me for praise and comfort.

I might not be practiced in giving those things, but I could be. For her.

Her first gown is elegant. Modest. A good dress to start with, since I've so thoroughly dented her confidence. I make her pose by the rocks; on the golden sand; and holding her hem up, ankle deep in the waves.

She's so stiff and unhappy, flinching at every instruction, that you'd think she'd never modeled before. I have to coax her into each photo, and it takes three times as long as it should to get a usable shot.

I say nothing. I've hurt her enough.

But when we walk back up the beach, her shorter legs hurrying ahead of mine, I sigh and check my watch. She hasn't spoken a single word since she arrived, and she's utterly wooden when she strikes each pose.

There are dozens more outfits. And who knows how many more hours of good light? At this rate, we won't get a third of the shoot done.

I toy with the idea of summoning another model at short notice. Strictly speaking, it's the most professional thing to do.

But the thought of the hurt and dismay on her face when I snapped at her earlier...

No. I won't do it. This is our model, and we'll make it work.

When we reach the huddle of whispering assistants, I snag Billie Blue's elbow and drag her aside. Out of earshot, where I can give her a little talk. Remind her of her job.

But when she looks up at me, her mouth pressed in a tight line and her expression resigned, that all falls away. I cup her face and breathe out a ragged sigh.

Coral

Archer Westbrook is touching my face. Cradling me like I'm precious.

Um. What?

I knock his hand away without thinking. He may be Billie's boss in this scenario, but he's a jerk. I don't want his hands on me.

Even if he really does look like a Norse god with his broad shoulders, leather jacket, and long blond hair scraped back with a hair tie.

Crap. My knees knock together under my gown. They don't make men like *this* in the baking videos I watch. He scowls, ducking his head and forcing me to meet his eye.

"I'm sorry about earlier," he murmurs, so only we can hear. His gray eyes hold mine, and I struggle to breathe.

I shrug one shoulder.

"Do you ever speak?"

It's my turn to scowl.

Yes, I want to say, *I speak to nice people. People who don't make my throat close up with nerves.*

He's already torn me apart for being a few pounds heavier than my sister. I'm not about to show him my stutter, too.

I clear my throat. Rehearse the words in my head to make sure, then whisper, slow and clear.

"Let's get back to work."

He growls with frustration, the sound gruff behind me, but I keep walking back to the garment rack.

I'm not an idiot. I can tell I'm a terrible model, but I promised Billie I'd try my best, so that's what I'll do.

The next dress is simpler, a work of draping white silks, with the tiniest braided straps over my shoulders. I wait while the seamstresses adjust for my curves, a hollow feeling in my gut.

I've never felt bad about my body before. I've always kind of liked the dip and swell of my form.

That's modeling, I guess. Especially with men like Archer around. No wonder Billie's so reluctant to eat my cupcakes.

Well, you know what? I prefer being a maid.

This time, when we walk down to the waves, I let my anger shine through my eyes. I raise my chin in challenge, my limbs still awkward, but not quite as wooden as last time. Archer hums behind his camera, snapping shot after shot.

"That's it. Better. Show me your spirit, Billie Blue."

When he lowers the camera, his eyes are dark and intense. They rake over me, taking in every inch of my body.

I can't help it. I cross my arms over my chest. Archer gusts out a sigh, shaking his head.

Whatever. If he doesn't want his models to be shy, he shouldn't be mean. I stick out my tongue and his eyebrows shoot up his forehead. His mouth twitches and he strolls over to me, his boots thudding over the damp sand, one hand tucked in his pocket.

He stops right in front of me. Close enough to touch. I could reach up and press my fingertip into the cleft of his chin. I could snatch his camera out of his grip and smash it on the sand.

"What on earth are you thinking about?" he murmurs. His voice is deep and smooth; it sends shivers skating over my skin. My nipples pebble under the thin, white satin against my crossed arms. His eyes flick down, and his mouth curls in a slow, knowing smile.

"Ah." He chuckles. "I see."

For the millionth time today, heat spreads over my cheeks. My eyes burn, and I blink back tears.

Why?

Why do I have to cry so easily?

And why is this man so hell bent on humiliating me?

I clear my throat, forcing the words out even as my face flushes even brighter.

"You are a cr-cruel man, Archer W-Westbrook."

His smirk falls, but it's too late. I turn around and stride back across the beach, not waiting to be dismissed, heading for the next garment bag with my head held high. The nice assistant Gavin gives me a questioning look, but I shake my head, keeping my arms crossed over my traitorous breasts.

Archer Westbrook already knows the effect he has on me.

I don't want every last person on this beach to know my humiliation.

* * *

We speed through the next few dresses, with Archer hardly

127

bothering to direct me. He's distracted, snapping pictures while barely looking through his camera lens. He seems more concerned with frowning at me, staring intently like I'm a riddle to be solved.

I roll my eyes, lifting the hem of a lacy knee-length bridal dress and stepping deeper into the waves. The cold water shocks my skin, zaps me with new energy, and I don't have to fake my exhilarated smile.

"Good," Archer murmurs, raising the camera to his eye. He snaps a series of photos, sea foam rushing around his boots. "Very good, sweetheart."

He has no right to call me that, but the name sends a secret thrill down my spine. Something pulses, hot and achy, between my legs.

I bite my lip, turning to give him my back, and gaze at him over my shoulder.

"Fuck," Archer mutters to himself.

I don't know if that's a good or bad thing, him cursing. He seems more worked up than angry, the corded muscles tight in his neck and his jaw grinding together. He grunts and adjusts his pants.

Oh. *Oh.* I flush red hot again, but this time I don't mind.

He wants me. The man who thinks I'm too big, who knows I can't model for shit—he wants my body. For a giddy moment, there's nothing but the hush of the sea and the gentle breeze. No people, no cry of seabirds, no *reality.*

I smirk straight into the camera lens. I don't know where this daring Coral came from, but I hope she never leaves.

"Jesus," he mutters, snapping several more photos. "I won't be able to sell any of these."

I slump.

Just like that, my newfound courage deserts me. Once again, I'm just the wrong twin sister, standing in someone else's dress, her feet numb in the sea.

"I don't mean it that way," Archer says quickly, as if he can read the defeat in my face. When he speaks again, it's quieter. Confessional. "I mean I don't want to share." His grip tightens on his camera where he holds it by his chest, his knuckles turning white. "I don't want anyone to see you like this. Only me."

My heart hammers in my chest as I process his words. It sounds like…

No, he *is* saying that. And not just with his words, but with his hungry eyes. Archer Westbrook is staring at me like a starving man at a feast.

I've never done anything like this. Never *felt* anything like this—an immediate connection to someone, sparks racing under my skin.

I lick my lips. "C-call me sweetheart again."

"Sweetheart," he purrs. I squeeze my thighs together, my breath catching in my throat. He watches every tiny movement of my body, reading my arousal in every twitch and gasp.

I've never been watched this closely before. Never been *seen* so fully.

It makes me want to show him more.

I glance over his shoulder, at the group of people clustered at the top of the beach. They're huddled around the coffee table, chatting. Their backs turned and their attention elsewhere.

I meet Archer's gaze and hook a thumb under my dress strap. He raises his camera again as I tug it down, showing my bare breast, and snaps a photo.

"Don't sh-show anyone," I warn him, cupping myself. I pinch

129

the nipple, tipping my head back with a gasp.

Archer chokes out a laugh.

"As if I could. I'd have to murder them on the spot just for looking at you."

My pussy throbs harder, slick and wanting between my thighs.

"Y-you don't mind my curves now."

He huffs out a breath. "Mind them? Sweetheart. You're the most beautiful woman I've ever seen."

There's no way that's true—the man works with freaking supermodels every day—but it's nice of him to say. Nicer than he's been all day. It warms me up to him just a tiny bit, and hunger claws at my belly when he reaches down again and palms the front of his jeans.

It should be crude. Off-putting.

But it makes my mouth water.

Already, through his dark jeans, I can see the outline of his cock. It's huge. A *statement*. A battering ram.

I squeeze my breast harder, biting my lip against a moan. Archer curses, glancing back over his shoulder.

"If we were alone," he tells me hurriedly, "I'd prove it to you. I'd lick your sweet pussy until you cried. For the *right* reasons this time."

Gavin's voice echoes down the beach, calling for us, and I yank my dress strap back up my shoulder, alarmed.

Archer looks rueful. Moody and impatient again, but not at me.

This time, he guides me back up the beach with his warm palm hovering over my back.

Half an inch of air. That's all there is between us. It makes me want to slam to a halt so his palm brushes my skin. I can almost feel his heat as it is, that tiny point of imagined contact sending warmth licking through my veins.

I come to a stop in front of the last garment bags. The lingerie.

Archer growls behind me.

Oh, god. Here we go.

Archer

❧

"Wait." I snake out a hand and grab Billie's wrist before she takes hold of the garment bag. The zipper is undone, the bag open to the breeze, and those tiny scraps of ivory satin and lace bring a roaring sound to my ears.

Her wrist is delicate in my grip. Her skin smooth and creamy. I rub my thumb over her pulse point, glaring around at the small crowd.

"Everybody go home."

"What?" Gavin splutters a laugh, his warm brown eyes crinkling at the corners. It occurs to me for the first time that my assistant is probably considered handsome.

My grip tightens on Billie.

"Did I stutter?" I snap, and I feel her flinch beside me. Fuck. When will I stop putting my foot in my mouth? She tugs her arm away, frowning down at the sand.

Gavin waves at the equipment, helpless.

"We still have four more outfits! The light's still good. Come on, Archer, we're on deadline."

All reasonable points. He's not saying anything untrue. But that doesn't stop me from pinning him with a murderous glare. Gavin shrinks back, baffled and alarmed, and everyone else around us holds their breath.

"Go," I grind out. My heartbeat thunders in my chest. "*Now.*"

They jerk into action, packing away tables and grabbing their things, shooting me worried glances and whispering together. Billie starts to move too, but I snag her by the shoulder.

"Not you. Gavin's right. We have work to do."

She doesn't question me. Doesn't ask why I've sent the others away and not her. She plucks up the first garment bag and ducks into the changing space, expression thoughtful.

I rub a palm over my chest as I wait for her to change, pacing back and forth. Will the lingerie fit? Maybe she needs these adjusted too. I didn't even think of that. And what the hell is wrong with my heart?

Fuck, I'm a mess.

When she steps back out with her robe wrapped tight around her, I swallow hard and face her. She tilts her head.

"Are you going to explain why you sent them away?"

Yeah, that's an easy one. I prowl over to her, only stopping with a few inches between our chests. She barely comes up to my chin.

"No one else can see you like this." I tug her robe open, eyes greedy, sucking in a deep breath at the bare expanses of milky skin. My eyes flick up to hers and she's watching me, pupils blown wide. "Only me. Do you understand?"

"You're very possessive."

And her stutter is gone. I don't point that out. Instead, I smirk, wrapping a red curl around my knuckle.

"You don't seem to mind, sweetheart."

133

She raises her chin. "You have no say in who I show myself to."

I want to beat my chest and roar.

"No," I croak. "Not yet."

But she must feel this too. This magnetic pull between us, drawing us together like the tide is pulled up the beach.

"I'm possessive too," she warns. Then her cheeks flush, and she ducks her head. "At least, I think I will be." She glares back up at me. "Are you prepared for that?"

Is she saying what I think she's saying? That she's… inexperienced?

Untouched and untried?

Jesus Christ. This girl is trying to kill me.

"Oh, I'm prepared." I slide a hand into her hair, cupping the side of her face. There are freckles dusting her pert little nose. "I'd like nothing better than you growling over me, sweetheart. Staking your claim."

I dip my head and drag the tip of my nose along her hairline, inhaling her scent. She smells like vanilla and cocoa powder. Warm cookies on a summer's day.

I nip her earlobe, smirking as she shudders. "I want you to rub your delicious scent *all over me.*"

Billie sucks in a shaky breath and pushes me away with gentle hands.

"Let's finish your shoot," is all she says.

It's not an answer. The evasion is maddening, but I grit my teeth and tilt my head down the beach.

Fine. We'll play this her way. Dancing around each other until she finally snaps.

I don't mind waiting her out.

I can be a very patient man.

* * *

The pop-up changing station is a set of three screens and a free-standing mirror listing to one side in the sand. Billie's clothes are tossed over the top of one screen, the sleeve of a thin emerald green sweater shifting in the breeze.

I'd been too wrapped up in preparations for the shoot to notice her outfit this morning. Her clothes are simple. Modest. Neat but worn-in. The sight of the faded patch on the knee of her jeans, of the loose thread on the collar of her sweater—it punches me in the solar plexus.

I clear my throat and knock on the wooden frame of the screen. Billie squeaks and staggers into the fabric wall, her corset half-fastened.

"May I?" I murmur. I don't know what I'll do if she says no. Dash my head against the rocks? But there's no need, my skull is safe, because Billie blows out a breath and gives me a quick nod.

She flaps a hand at the row of hooks running down her spine. "I c-can't do them up."

I hum, stepping closer. "They can be tricky."

It's meant to be comforting, a peace offering, but she squints at me like she's trying to find the insult.

There isn't one. I don't know how I managed to go so badly wrong with this angel, but she's flawless. A walking work of art. The first set of lingerie took ten years off my life.

"Maybe it's too small," she whispers, frowning at the mirror, her mouth twisted. No. Hell no. I'm not letting this happen again.

"It's perfect." I pause behind her, hooking the corset up smoothly. It's a cruel joke—the last thing I want to do is fasten her *into* the lingerie. I'd rather rip it clean in two, sending hooks flying to the sand.

It takes a few seconds to do up the corset, but I linger. Her soft expanses of skin make my chest ache. The corset nips her in at the waist, emphasizing the mouthwatering swells of her body.

I breathe in deeply through my nose.

Cupcakes. Holy shit.

"D-do you always help the models dress?"

I bark out a laugh. "No. Never."

She meets my eye in the mirror. Raises her chin.

"Why me?"

My hand rests on her shoulder, then slides around to cup her neck. It's not a threat—it's a caress, my thumb skating over the vulnerable places beneath her jaw.

She sighs and melts back against my chest. My heart lunges at my rib cage, trying to smash its way through to her.

I dip my head and speak with my lips pressed directly to her temple.

"*Why you*? Don't you know? Haven't I made it very fucking clear?" I pulse my grip on her throat, just enough to make her eyelashes flutter. "You own me, sweetheart."

* * *

You know what?

Screw being patient.

Billie Blue Walsh is trying to murder me.

She wades into the surf, her robe wrapped tight around her middle. The frothy waves break against her legs, and goosebumps ripple over her skin. It's midday now, the sun shining bronze in her hair, and licking warmth all over her body.

She turns around, fixes me with a wry look, then shrugs her robe off and tosses it to me.

I catch it, the thin fabric still warm from her body, and press it to my nose, breathing her in.

She rolls her eyes. "You're playing this up."

Does she think I'm exaggerating how badly I want her? The words drip out of me, voice low.

"I promise you I'm not. Your scent is addictive. I wish I could bottle you and spray you on my pillow."

She's flushed pink and pleased as she cocks one hip, posing in the third set of bridal lingerie. There's even a scrap of lace around one thigh, a garter, and the thought of tearing it off with my teeth makes my head spin.

Billie snorts. "You're supposed to take photos."

Right. My whole career. My whole reason for existence, before I saw her. It's fallen out of my brain, replaced by her intoxicating presence.

I raise my camera and snap photo after photo, not bothering to tell her that I'd rather sell my kidney than these pictures of her.

These will just be for me. The designer can hire someone else to finish the shoot.

"Aren't you going to direct me?" She tosses her hair over one shoulder.

Fuck yes. I'd like nothing more.

"Seduce me," I growl. "These clothes are for a wedding night. Look at me like I'm your new husband."

"You mean look at the camera." Her mouth twitches in amusement, even as she strokes her fingertips down the center of her chest, over her smooth, soft stomach.

"If you like," I mutter, raising the camera and watching her through the lens instead. I zoom in, taking in every freckle, every inch of her body in high definition.

Her fingertips graze the top of her panties.

I breathe in hard through my nose. "Fuck."

Her middle finger dips inside. Just the first knuckle.

"*Do it*," I beg.

I've never been a man to ask nicely. To flatter and plead. But to see this woman touch herself, to hear the soft moans of her arousal—I would live my whole life on my knees.

She tucks another finger inside the waistband, but won't go any deeper. Not to where her pussy must be clenching down on nothing, slick and wanting.

I could fill her up. With my hands, cock and tongue. Make that ache go away.

"Show me, then," I rasp, and to my shock, she complies. She draws her fingers out, then tugs her panties to the side.

Her pussy is pink and swollen, dusted with red hair, and I can't help the groan that escapes me.

"Is that for me?" I ask, reaching down to palm my cock. I've been hard all morning, stiff to the point of pain.

"It depends." She runs a fingertip up her slit, just on the surface. "What would you do with it?"

"Worship it," I say immediately. "Worship *you*. Until you scream so loud your lungs burst."

She hums, circling the sensitive bead of her clit.

"That doesn't sound comfortable."

"Comfort is overrated."

She laughs, a little hiccup of a sound.

I fall to my knees in the sand, placing the camera and her

robe at my side.

"Come here," I tell her. Billie darts a look around the beach, at the houses lining the cliffs above us, but there's no one here. We're alone with the waves.

A drumbeat starts in my chest as she walks to me slowly, the sea water sloshing around her legs. Her teeth dig into her plump, pink bottom lip, and I reach for her, impatient. She gasps as I yank her closer.

My hands dwarf her hips. She's a doll compared to me—albeit a doll with luscious curves. The swell of her hips, her ample breasts straining against her bra...

I snarl, burying my face in her stomach. My tongue swipes a long line up her body, tasting her from her belly button to her bra, and she gasps and clutches my shoulders.

Yes. This is what I want. Her holding on to me for dear life as I consume her, as I swallow her whole.

"You're *mine*," I mutter, sliding my hands around to squeeze her ass. I bring one palm down on her ass cheek, making her jump and squeak.

The wet spot on her panties grows in front of my eyes.

"Yeah." I rub the spot I just spanked, soothing the sting away. "You like that, don't you sweetheart?"

She hums, tipping her head back, swaying in my hold. I hook her leg over my shoulder.

"Tell me you want my mouth on your pussy."

I speak the words a hair's breadth from her panties, my warm breath washing over the lace. She moans, already quaking, scrabbling at my head, my neck, my shoulders.

"Y-yes. I want your mouth on my p-pussy."

Triumph swells and bursts in my chest, searing hot through my whole body, and I snarl as I bury my face between her legs.

I mouth and suck at her through the lace, teasing her until she sobs.

A small hand bats at my head.

"D-do it *properly*."

I grin, tugging her panties aside with my teeth.

"Say please."

"*Archer—*"

I plunge my tongue into her folds. She's everything I imagined and more—hot and slick and deliciously tangy, quivering with need. She moans and writhes, so fucking responsive that I can't help but thrust my hips against the air. Even on my knees, she's so small compared to me. Delicate and light.

"Have you ever come before, sweetheart?" I speak with my mouth pressed in her core, the vibration humming through her.

"I don't... I don't know." She sounds far away. Dazed.

I swirl my tongue around her clit. "You'd know."

She mutters something, but I don't catch it. I'm too busy losing myself in her taste, her scent, her wet warmth. I want her all over me, from my eyebrows to my chin. I want to stamp a claim on her the way she's claimed me. I rub around her entrance without dipping inside, my finger broad against her tight pussy.

What would that feel like, wrapped around my cock?

I shake my head and lick her deeper, my brain fried.

For a girl who's never come before, she doesn't hold back now. She climbs swiftly and easily, as natural as breathing, her pleasure cresting as she writhes in my arms. She jerks her hips, riding my face, and I hum my approval and smack her ass.

Yes, I want to tell her. *Use me. Take me, too.*

"Arch... Archer..." She comes with a breathless squeak, her limbs turning to jelly beneath her. I hold her up, licking her through it until she collapses in my arms, breathing hard. I tuck her across my lap, brushing her hair out of her face.

Billie peers up at me, squinting out of one eye.

I grin down at her, my chin slick and shining.

Hearing her snort of amusement makes my chest ache. I tuck her closer, running my palms over every inch I can reach.

I've found her. The woman I've been waiting for. *My* woman.

I screw my eyes shut and I swear to myself—I'll never let her go.

Coral

I sit cradled on Archer's lap, his hard, muscled thighs supporting my weight like it's nothing.

I'm done. I'm cooked. My brain has left the building.

When the rumble of the waves and the cry of seabirds finally pierces my daze, I clear my throat and struggle to my feet. I have to tug my panties back so they cover me, the lace soaked and ruined, and heat floods down from my hairline.

"Oh no you don't." Archer pushes to his feet, cradling my cheek and brushing his thumb over my lip. "Don't go blushing and feeling ashamed. You're beautiful, Billie Blue."

My sister's name on his lips is like a bucket of icy water tipped down my back.

Archer thinks I'm *her*. A successful model at the start of a dazzling career. A brave, shining presence—not a maid who hides away in her apartment.

He touched me, put his mouth *there*, and he doesn't even know who I am.

Crap.

I stumble back up the beach, my mind racing as he strolls by my side. All his earlier moodiness is long gone. He's smiling and peaceful, the sunshine glinting golden in his tied back blond hair. I must have pulled a few strands from their tie when I grabbed his face, rode his tongue, because they dangle now beside his sturdy cheekbones.

Snatching my robe from Archer's hand as we walk, I shove my shaking hands through the sleeves and tug it around me. He frowns at me, concerned, but I avoid his eye.

Oh god. Oh *god*. He'll be so angry.

He'll look at me like he did this morning.

With disappointment and anger in his eyes.

I can't bear it. I *won't*. Not when what we just did together was the most magical experience of my life. Maybe I'm a coward—okay, I'm definitely a coward—but I just *know* that I'll never feel like that again.

I can't ruin the memory that I'll hold close for my whole life.

And this day has been about Billie, about her career and about not letting Archer and the designer down.

So I'll be selfish. Just this once.

I'll protect my heart.

Archer strides ahead when we reach the makeshift work station, grabbing a bottle of water and swigging from it thirstily. I watch the column of his throat bobbing, hypnotized, before I shake myself and grab the next garment bag.

He gives me a small smile as I walk past to the changing area. There's so much trust and hope in his eyes.

My chest cleaves in two as I duck behind the divider. As I pull on my own clothes with trembling hands instead of the next lingerie set, and pause to suck in one last breath.

I can almost smell him. My screaming emotions conjure his

scent—the crisp, masculine scent that surrounded me on his lap. I close my eyes, feeling the ghost of his touch on my skin, my heart shattering inside me.

It's easy to sneak out. I slip through a gap in the changing stall, hurrying away across the beach with my ragged breath loud in my ears.

I've just reached my battered old car, tucked in beside the sidewalk at the top of the beach, when a roar splits the sky. Archer stands frozen on the sand, his expression broken as he watches me tug open my car door.

I throw myself into the driver's seat, risking one last glimpse through the window.

His chest heaves, the movement so stark I can see it from all the way off the beach. Archer takes one step toward me but stumbles to a halt, a hand reaching.

Like he can't believe I'd do this. That I'd run away and leave him behind after what we just shared.

He doesn't know a single thing I'm capable of.

He doesn't even know who I am.

* * *

Billie is sprawled on the sofa in my maid's tunic when I get home, her usually cheerful face drawn and sad.

"Hey," she murmurs as I walk inside, my shoulders slumping all the way down to the floorboards. She does a double-take. "You look how I feel."

I nod, too exhausted to speak. My shoes trail sand across our living room, and I kick them off before flopping down on the rug beside the sofa.

Billie scratches at my scalp as I tip my head back on the

cushions.

"You want to talk about it?"

"Nope. You?"

She huffs out a breath. "No." Then: "What a day."

I hum in agreement, my eyes drifting closed. Though my heart is aching and raw, at least I'm *here*. In our quiet sanctuary, filled with sunshine and potted plants. The art prints we picked out together at a flea market hang on the walls, and Billie's got soft music playing.

"What's the verdict?" She tugs at a loose thread on the sofa cushion. "You gonna be a model with me, Coral?"

I snort, turning my head to meet her eye. She bites her lip, holding back a laugh, and suddenly the day's humiliation doesn't seem so bad. I throw up my hands, ranting at the ceiling.

"I sucked! I was so, so bad. The clothes were all too small, and I swear, I had the charisma of drying paint. Archer could barely—"

I cut myself off, my throat tightening. I don't want to talk about him.

"Yeah," Billie whispers, playing with my hair with her good hand. "It's rough out there. For maids, too."

"Oh god," I groan. "What did you do?"

"Nothing!" she squawks. Billie is a terrible liar.

"Did you break something valuable?"

"No…"

"Did you piss Mr. Koven off?"

She chews on her lip, face guilty.

"Um. Maybe. In a way."

I nod, dropping my head back and staring at the ceiling. The sunlight plays over the white paint, tiny shadows dancing where the potted plants sway by the open windows.

I can hardly be angry. Whatever she did to my boss, I sure as hell did worse to hers. Jeez—I rode his face; ground my pussy onto his tongue; moaned out his name. Guilt floods my insides, rising hot up my throat, and I swallow hard.

How could I do this to her? It's like I was a whole other person today. Someone who gets caught up in the moment, hazy with lust, and puts her sister's career in danger.

I reach for Billie's good hand and squeeze her fingers.

I'll tell her. I will. I'll tell her everything.

All the shameful things I've done.

But not today. Not when everything feels so sore and sad. I'll take one night to lick my wounds, to gather my courage, and I'll confess tomorrow.

Hopefully my twin sister can forgive me.

Hopefully I can forgive *myself.*

* * *

Our phones start buzzing as we clear up after dinner, washing the plates and wiping down the table in tired silence. I ignore my phone at first, watching the screen light up as it rattles against the coffee table, then turning away.

It buzzes once for a text. Twice. Three times.

Then it starts to ring.

"Crap." I wipe my hands on the dish cloth and toss it on the counter. But Billie squawks and rushes across the room, swiping up my phone before I can get there first.

"Billie?"

She shakes her head, staring down at my phone, horrified. She stands there, holding my phone as it buzzes in her palm, until finally it stops.

Silence rings through the apartment.

"Billie, what—"

Her phone chirps on the kitchen counter, the screen lighting up with a text. I whip my head around, trepidation sliding down my spine.

It buzzes again.

And again.

"Oh my god." I dash across the kitchen, bumping my hip against the table, and snatch her phone up with a shaking hand. Sure enough, Archer's name lights up the screen as it rings again in my palm. "I d-don't... I can't..."

Billie clears her throat. She holds up her palms, my phone tucked in her fingers of my good hand, her cast bulky on the other. My phone keeps buzzing, the screen a glowing blue rectangle in her grip.

"Maybe..." she twists her mouth, but keeps talking. "Maybe we could swap phones for the night. No questions asked?"

I'm nodding before she's finished her sentence.

"Yes," I gasp. "Th-that sounds good."

She frowns slightly, concerned. I hardly ever stutter when it's just us two, alone.

But we're not alone, are we? Apparently we have two ticking time bombs in our hands.

"Coral, is everything alright—"

"You s-said no questions!" I dodge around the side of the table, her phone tucked close to my chest. It keeps buzzing there, rattling my aching heart through my rib cage. "I'm going to bed."

She nods, even though it's still light out. "Okay. Um. Me too."

We shut ourselves away in our bedrooms, a thousand unanswered questions hanging thick in the air.

Tomorrow. We'll sort through all this tomorrow.

I blow out a breath, my shoulder blades pressed to my door, and stare down at Billie's phone in my palm. It buzzes against my skin, the screen lit with his name, and when I swipe to answer, my throat clamps tight.

"Hello?" I croak, dread sliding through my gut. "Archer?"

There's a sigh down the line.

Then: "You owe me a photo shoot, sweetheart."

Archer

I've never claimed to be a good man.

If the only way she'll see me again is to finish the job she was hired to do, then fine. I'll press whatever advantage I have, pull whatever strings I can, if it means being near her.

I'm not proud, but I can't bring myself to care, either. I'll do *anything* for a chance to convince my girl she's mine. I don't know where I went wrong earlier, and I've played every second of the day over and over in my head.

Whatever I did, whatever I said, I'll fix it.

I have to.

I need her.

It's ridiculous to be this addicted to someone I only met this morning. I know how fucking crazy I sound. But here's the thing—*I don't care.*

I'm Archer Westbrook. I've never given a shit what other people think of me, and I'm sure as hell not going to start now. I don't care if I seem whipped, if I have to throw myself at her feet.

Hers is the only opinion that matters. The only one I want to hear.

Maybe I spooked her. Moved too fast. The thought makes my chest seize, but if that's the problem, I'll promise we'll go slow. We can take as long as she needs, just as long as she doesn't push me away.

When she chokes out her agreement over the phone, she doesn't sound like she wants to see me. Her voice is thick with dread.

We arrange to meet in a little cove, further along the coast. It's more sheltered than the beach, away from prying eyes, with lanterns lining the path to the water and a crystal clear waterfall. The light will be shit for photos, but I don't care.

I just need to see her.

I get there early, my camera clenched tight in my grip as I stride along the stone path. The cove is quiet, the only sounds the distant lap of waves and the sighing breeze. It's a warm night, warm and muggy, and a bead of sweat trickles down my spine.

What if she doesn't come?

I take a few photos to distract myself, playing with the different settings to try and capture the pink evening light. I almost miss the quiet footsteps padding along the path behind me.

"Archer." My heart stops. I turn slowly, the hairs raising on my skin.

She's here. My girl. Her red hair is braided over one shoulder, and she looks… different. Tired and *gaunt*.

Billie smiles at me, but it's empty. Distant. She shifts her jacket in her arms, and that's when I notice the cast. It wraps around her wrist, clunky and awkward, wound with white bandages. I let out a groan, rushing over, my boots slamming heavy on the stone path.

"What happened?" I touch her face, her arms, her shoulders, checking for more signs of damage. How the hell did she get hurt in the space of a few hours?

Billie Blue steps back, away from my roaming hands. I shove them in my pockets instead, my chest caving in.

She really doesn't want me. Doesn't feel what I feel.

It was all in my head.

And it *must* have been, because that unstoppable magnetic pull I felt toward her earlier—it's gone. I look at her now, and I feel nothing.

God. I'm going insane. It's the only explanation.

"I got hit by a cyclist." Even her *voice* sounds different. Surer. "It's just a sprain. But, um. I obviously can't finish the shoot."

"No." I stare down at her cast, something screaming in the back of my brain. There's something off here, something I'm missing. "No, I see that."

"Archer." She wets her lip, a hint of that blush returning to her cheeks. "About what happened earlier…it can't happen again. I'm trying to start a career."

I nod vaguely. I don't even try to argue. Because even though nothing's changed, even though it makes no sense… right now, I don't even want her.

Fuck. Am I so fickle? I'd been *sure.* I'd wanted to marry her, for fuck's sake. To take her home and never let her go.

Now the woman in front of me is a stranger.

"Did…" I shake my head. "Did something happen? You seem so different, sweetheart."

Please say yes, I beg her privately. *Please help me make sense of this.*

"Nothing happened." She sounds kind of strangled. She's an awful liar. "I'm just not interested, Archer. I'm sorry."

"Alright," I say slowly, stepping aside to let her leave. I watch her walk away, my gut churning, but unlike when I watched her run away earlier, there's no urge to follow.

There's only the rasp of my breath.

A dull ache in my chest.

And something screaming in my brain for attention.

Coral

I haven't cried like this since I was sixteen and our family cat died. The sobs wrack my whole body, scouring my throat raw for hours until I finally hiccup to a stop, exhausted. I curl deeper into my blankets, mushing my face into the pillow, a hollow ache pulsing through my chest.

God, this *day*. What a disaster.

Billie and I came crashing out of our bedrooms right after our phone calls. She was chalky white, deep shadows bruising her eyes, and I was no better.

We confessed in stilted whispers. No details, but the vague problem. We'd both gotten tangled up with each other's boss.

Neither man knew our real identities.

We were screwed. Caught up in our own lies, our hearts breaking in tandem. Well, we're twin sisters. We do a lot of stuff together, but this was a new one.

In the end, the solution was easy. Horribly simple. Billie set out to meet Archer in my place, while I called Mr. Koven by video chat so he wouldn't see my two good arms. We did the other's dirty work, turning down the men so they'd never discover our lies.

My normally unruffled boss was wrecked. Torn apart by one day with my sister. I hung up when it was done, tossing my phone on my bed spread and bursting into tears.

Such a mess. So many hurt feelings. All because Billie and I swapped places.

I sniffle, tugging my blanket higher over my shoulder. I can't help but torture myself, wondering what might have happened if I'd met Archer properly. As *myself*, as Coral. The shy, curvy twin.

Would he even have noticed me? Would he have called me sweetheart and found excuses to touch me the way he did today?

Or was it the supermodel he wanted all along? Billie Blue, the beautiful, confident twin.

Thoughts of Archer make my heart throb in my chest. It feels so sore, like it's been stewing in sea water just like my legs.

Will he be upset when she turns him down? Angry? Will he ever think of me after this?

I bury my face in the pillow, groaning. I know down to the marrow in my bones—I'll think of Archer every single day.

* * *

The knocking starts just after midnight. A frantic pounding on our front door, the sound echoing through the still rooms. I squint at the lit up screen of my alarm clock, my eyes blurry from crying.

Is it Billie? I never heard her come home. I push myself

upright, swinging my legs out of bed. My limbs ache like I'm a thousand years old as I hobble across the room, tugging my robe off the door hook.

"I'm coming!" I call, even though the knocker won't hear me over their racket.

What if Billie's hurt again? The memory of getting that text, of reading she was in the hospital, makes my blood run cold.

I don't know what I'd do without my sister. Especially now, when I've pushed the only man I've ever felt drawn to away.

Archer...

It can't be him. It won't. I refuse to get my hopes up. I knot the belt of my robe tightly at my waist, shuffling out of my bedroom into the shadowed apartment.

It looks different at night. The plants cast weird shadows, and moonlight spreads over the floorboards in silver pools. The wood creaks under my feet as I creep across the rug, wincing at the steady banging.

Whoever it is, they're going to wake up our neighbors. I push back my shoulders and throw open the door.

"Do you know what time it..."

I trail off, stunned. Archer stands in the doorway, gripping both sides of the frame. His jaw is clenched tight, and his eyes are dark as they flick over my body, checking both my wrists.

He scowls.

"I thought so. You have some explaining to do, sweetheart."

My grip flexes on the door. I could slam it in his face. It would serve him right, coming here in the middle of the night, banging on our door loud enough to wake the dead. Digging up our address from god knows where. Except...

Except there's hurt beneath the anger in his eyes. Hurt and confusion.

155

Archer looks baffled.

"You're not Billie Blue. Why did you lie to me?" he rasps.

I shrug miserably, waving a hand down myself.

"Billie hurt her arm. She couldn't do the shoot, but she couldn't lose the opportunity either. So, um. She sent me."

He nods along, impatient. His blond hair looks silver in the moonlight. It's out of his tie, hanging over his broad shoulders.

Shoulders that I clung to just a few hours ago. That I dug my nails into and rocked my hips against.

"Yeah, I guessed *that*." He rakes a hand through that hair. "But afterwards. When it was the two of us. Why didn't you tell me? Why did you *run?*"

I can't do this. I can't have this conversation. I've had it so many times before—with disappointed parents and teachers and speech therapists, all those people who rooted for me and I let down, even though I tried my best.

So I deflect, pushing back at him.

"How did you find out?" I raise my chin, trying to mimic his confidence. His control. "And why did you come here?"

Archer scrubs a hand over his mouth, stepping back. The way he's looking at me—it's like I'm a stranger. Like he doesn't know me at all.

My bruised heart crumples into a ball.

Time slows down as I watch him shake his head. As I watch bitterness twist his mouth as he turns to leave.

"Wait." I dart forward, grabbing the sleeve of his black sweater. He stills, vibrating with tension—like a battle horse held in check by flimsy reins. "D-don't go. I'm sorry."

His skin is hot through his sleeve. His arm is sculpted, deliciously bulky, like he's used to lifting far heavier things than cameras. I tug lamely on the fabric.

"I d-didn't think you'd want me," I whisper at his boots. "Not when you found out who I really am. I'm not a model, Archer. I'm a maid."

He blows out a slow breath. He turns back to face me, his big leather boots pointing at my bare toes.

"Something didn't seem right when I saw your sister." His voice is dull. Robotic. "Part of me knew it wasn't you. So I found her on social media, and in one of her photos, there you were." He bites out a harsh laugh. "The woman I'd lost my mind over."

I tug on his sleeve again, but he stays put. Immovable. And when he keeps talking, his words are curt.

"The two of you must have had a good laugh."

"It wasn't like that."

"No?"

I shake my head, tears brimming. When I risk a glance up at him, one spills over and rolls down my cheek.

Just like that, his ice melts. Archer ducks his head, fussing over me, cradling my face and wiping away the stray tear. He looks horrified to see me cry, cursing himself out under his breath.

"Wait. No. Shit. Don't be sad, sweetheart. Fuck—I keep doing this. What the hell."

"I'm sorry!" I wail, backing up into the apartment. Archer follows, kicking the door shut behind him. "Y-you're right to be mad. I would be too."

"Okay, well, I'm done with that now. It's over with. So there's no need to cry, alright?"

I nod, even as more tears slide down my face. Archer casts around wildly, then ushers me back to the sofa.

"Sit here. Shall I—shall I get you something? A glass of

water?"

"N-no thank you." I plop down onto the sofa cushions, my arms wrapped around my waist. "You don't have to stay," I tell my knees.

Archer pauses. The apartment is quiet. His next question is so careful.

"Do you want me to go?"

"*No.*" I tear at the loose thread on the cushion. "I never want you to go again."

It's too much, too honest, way too intense for someone I only just met today. I cringe, waiting for him to mutter some excuse and leave. To get away from my crazy.

Instead, Archer lets out a ragged sigh. It's the sound of pure *relief*. He crouches in front of me, his big fingers so gentle as they tuck a stray piece of hair behind my ear.

"Why don't we circle back," he murmurs. The moonlight sparkles in his gray eyes. "You thought I wouldn't want you because you're a maid. Is that right?"

I hiccup. "Uh-huh."

"Bullshit," he says immediately. "I'd want you whatever your job. I'd want you even if you worked knee-deep in garbage all day."

I giggle, wincing as it turns into a watery snort.

"Now, the most important question…" Archer tips onto his knees, the thud echoing through the floorboards as he leans forward to drag his mouth up my neck. "What's it like, exactly—your maid costume? Paint me a picture."

I huff, even as I can't keep the smile off my face.

"It's a uniform, not a costume. It's not like my boss makes me clean in a skimpy little French maid outfit."

"Good." Archer nibbles my earlobe. "That's one less man I

have to kill."

I hesitate, then place my hands on his collarbone. Gingerly, like he might explode upright at any moment. When he hums and stays put, I run my palms over his shoulders, biting my lip. His scent is everywhere, surrounding me, and I want to drown in it.

"Are there many on the list? Men you need to kill."

"Hundreds. Thousands. All the men who ever looked at you and wanted you for themselves."

"I don't think—"

"Believe me, sweetheart." He licks a stripe over my pulse point. Heat pulses through my core. "There are *thousands*." He shakes his head sadly. "They shouldn't have to die. But life can be cruel."

He's *funny*, my photographer. Surprisingly playful given how thunderous he'd looked this morning, striding around and barking orders at the beach. He laughs when I tell him so, tossing back his head and exposing the thick column of his throat.

I've been thinking about that throat all day, ever since I watched him drain that water bottle.

I lunge forward and suck a bruise on it while I can.

The room changes. The air crackles with energy, and my breathing stutters. Archer rocks back on his heels.

"You left me aching, sweetheart."

I nod, stealing glimpses at his lap. The hard outline of his cock juts along the leg of his jeans. My abdomen twists, my nerve endings zapping under my skin.

"I'm sorry," I murmur. My fingers itch to reach for him. To hold the length of him in my palm.

"I won't rush you, sweet girl. But I'd give *anything* to sink my cock deep inside you." My breath rushes out of me as his mouth quirks. "Would you like that?"

Would I like that?

I squirm on the sofa cushion, hot and restless, already whimpering at his words.

"Archer. Yes."

Archer

I push to my feet, a thousand urgent impulses clamoring for my attention.

I want to tug off that robe and suck on her rosy nipples.

I want to get her tiny hand wrapped around my cock.

A vision of her bare ass resting on my lap, my palm cracking down and leaving pink hand prints drifts across my mind, but there's no time to make it happen.

Because she's tugging down my zipper. Popping the button of my jeans. And fishing out my cock all by herself. Sitting on the edge of the sofa, her pert little nose is level with the head, and she darts out her pink tongue, lapping at me like a cat.

Fuck. *Fuck.*

"Wait, wait." She stops, blinking up at me. I push my thumb between her lips and she sucks me in, swirling her tongue until I groan. I rub it along her tongue, relishing the soft heat. "I still don't know your name, sweetheart."

She lets go of me with a pop.

"Coral," she says, voice husky. Her mouth quirks. "Our

parents were hippies."

Coral. It suits her. She looked kind of like a mermaid with her wild red hair at the beach, walking into the waves.

"Are you going to lick me, Coral?"

"Uh-huh." She pulls my cock back to her lips, tracing them like lipstick. "It's my turn to make you cry."

I open my mouth to respond but she sucks me deep inside, sinking several inches into her sweet, warm mouth. Her hand works the base as she suckles on the head of my cock, her head bobbing and her tongue swirling.

She may be inexperienced, but she's a goddamn natural.

"Shit." I bury my hands in her hair. I can't help it; my hips twitch forward, thrusting until I hit the back of her throat. Coral hums, the vibrating rattling all the way through to my teeth, slurping me deeper as I plunge my cock inside her.

"Shit," I say again. All other words are gone. "Fuck. *Sweetheart.* That mouth. That fucking mouth."

She moans, bobbing her head eagerly, her spare hand drifting down to squeeze her own breast through her robe.

"Yeah, that's it. You like this, sweetheart? You like sucking down your man?"

She hums louder, her hand dropping to her lap, nudging the robe aside to delve between her thighs. That's what breaks me. Catching a glimpse of her tiny soaked panties.

There will be time for blow jobs. *Years*—hell, the rest of our lives, if I have any say in it.

Right now, I need something else. I need to wedge myself deep inside her.

"Come here."

She pulls off just in time for me to scoop her up, turning us both and crashing back on the sofa. Coral lands on my lap, bouncing on my thighs, the creamy mounds of her tits swelling and falling.

I tear open her robe, snarling at what I find: the perfect body. Curvy and sinful. I thought I must have imagined it, back on the beach. Built it up in my own head, but here it is again.

Paradise.

Her nightgown whips over her head before she can blink. I trace a line down the center of her chest with one callused finger, down her soft stomach, dipping into her belly button.

"God." I gather her breasts in each hand, squeezing them together. I want to fuck her there too. "You're a wet dream. A work of art." My grip tightens and she whimpers. "Tell me you're mine."

"I'm yours," she whispers, color bright on her cheeks. Then she adds, voice stronger: "And you're *mine*, Archer Westbrook. Mine to fuck. Mine to love."

I never expected language like that from my shy sweetheart, nor the jealous bite to her voice. My cock swells impossibly harder between us.

She pushes onto her knees without urging, notching me at her entrance.

"I haven't done this before," she tells me, then sinks down three inches like she hasn't just blown my mind.

I knew that about her.

I did.

But fuck if that doesn't send heating surging through me. My hips twitch up, impaling her deeper, and Coral gasps, her head rolling on her neck.

She's *tight*. Warm and wet, pulsing around me.

"How does it feel?" I grit out, fisting her hair in one hand and squeezing her thigh with the other. "Does it hurt?"

163

She bites her lip, thinking about it, then shakes her head slowly.

"It doesn't hurt. It feels tight, it's stretching me, but... but..."

"*What?*" I'll die without the end of that sentence.

"It's *so good*," she moans.

"Good." I thrust up harder, feeding her another inch. "Because it's the last cock you'll ever have. I never want you out of my fucking sight."

"Don't you trust me?" she murmurs dreamily. Her head lolls as she begins to work up and down, sliding on my shaft. Her eyes are glazed, peering up at me, her arms winding around my neck.

I tug my handful of her hair.

"Of course I trust you. But I'll fucking die if I don't get between your legs every day. I need you with me. Within reach."

She's nodding in agreement, hiccuping and gasping, and she's so honest in her pleasure, so needy and wound tight, my heart clenches in my chest.

I love her. I love her so fucking much.

"I don't care that it's so soon." I pulse my hips up as I talk, and she sinks further down on me with every bounce in my lap. "I love you. Coral. You're mine."

"I'm yours," she breathes, slamming all the way down to the hilt. I'm filling her up, stretching her pussy, her muscles quivering over every inch of my cock. "I need you too. I feel so—so desperate for you. As soon as you stop touching me, I want to scream." Her eyes slam shut, and her hips stutter. "Oh, god. *Archer*. It's happening again."

I tug on her hair, pulling her head to the side, and scrape my teeth over her neck.

"Let it happen, sweetheart."

Feeling her come from the inside out—that's what fucking miracles are made of. The pressure starts and builds, her channel spasming, then she clamps down on my cock like a vice. She rides me through it all, movements frantic, head tossed back and moaning loud, and her pussy twitches when I crack a palm against her ass.

She ends on the tiniest squeak.

I want to record it next time.

I want it for my fucking ring tone.

"God, baby." I pump my hips up, ears ringing. "So sexy. You're so goddamn sexy."

Heat floods inside her as I come, emptying into her pussy with a groan, my forehead pressed into her shoulder. It takes forever, dredging up spurt after spurt, and a wicked voice in my brain whispers that she might get pregnant.

I thrust up harder, just in case. You know, to help it along. She's still squirming in my lap, working herself up again, and I'm right there with her.

I'll never get enough.

Not even if I fuck her every day for the rest of our lives.

Better get started.

Coral

꧁꧂

Two years later

My husband likes to take photos of me.

Intimate photos.

Sometimes he wanders into the bathroom in our house on the cliffs, the windows overlooking the beach where we first met. I'll be stretched out in the tub, chin deep in bubbles, and he'll wink at me as he raises his camera. I'll smirk and prop my heel on the tub, showing off my bare, soapy leg.

Sometimes he finds me when I'm dressing. Hooking my bra strap into place; tugging the scraps of my lacy panties up my thighs; the soft light of our walk-in closet painting me gold.

He sinks down to his knees, eyes hungry behind the lens, and tells me to seduce him. To show the camera what I've got.

Sometimes I'll flick open one of the books in his office and a photo of me will slither out. They're everywhere in this house—inside books, propped on shelves, beneath Archer's pillow. Some arty, some erotic. The most intimate, he hides

166

away, just in case prying eyes come over for dinner.

He can't get enough. He calls me his muse. The only woman he ever wants to photograph.

The day after we met, he stopped photographing models. It was always professional for him, but even so—he says his inspiration has moved elsewhere.

Now he photographs beaches and landscapes. Bright festivals and cultural events.

And me. Always me.

I smooth a palm over the hard swell of my belly. Soon there will be more of us to photograph.

"What are you doing?" Archer's warm voice slides around me, enveloping me like honey. I pause at the kitchen counter, smiling down at the cupcake I'm icing. His hands grip the counter on either side of my waist.

"Working on a new design."

He hums, trailing his lips up my neck.

There's one more thing Archer photographs—the designs for my cake decorating business. His gorgeous photos are half the reason it's such a success, though he'd never let me say that.

"All work and no play." Archer tuts, gripping my earlobe between his teeth and tugging gently. Heat flares in my core, an ache building in my clit.

"What are you going to d-do about it?"

These days, I only stutter around Archer when he turns me on.

So, you know. All the freaking time.

His palm smacks against my ass without warning, and I jump, squeezing the edge of the counter. I nudge my legs apart, rocking my hips back against his jeans, and Archer chuckles, the sound smoky in my ear.

"So eager." He thrusts against me, his length hard against my ass. "You're wearing me thin, sweetheart."

I huff out a laugh. "Poor baby."

"I know." I can hear the grin in his voice. "But what a way to go."

It can't be real. Sometimes I think that. There's no way anyone can be this lucky, this happy, this deep in love.

But then Archer proves me wrong every single time, squashing every doubt before it has time to fester.

He loves me, this handsome photographer. The Norse god with the camera. He's mine.

And I am his.

I turn in his arms and prove it to him.

IV

Fake Maid

Eli

Bed rest.

Bed rest.

What am I, one thousand years old? Bed rest is for the elderly and infirm; for feverish children who can't lift their limbs. Not a thirty-one year old man who climbs mountains and runs ultra-marathons to relax. Who has taken more spills on the cliff than most people take on the stairs.

Bed rest. *Please.* If I weren't so insulted, I'd find it funny.

Of course, the problem with hiring the best surgeons in the land is that they have egos to match. And that was the devil's bargain I struck in my desperation to get better quickly: Doctor Price would fix my mangled hand, but only if I followed his instructions to the letter. And when he reluctantly agreed that 'bed rest' could mean 'house rest'…

In hindsight, after three days trapped in my mansion, it was not worth it. Better to have chanced it with any old doctor. Hell—better to have splinted the damn thing myself.

This is a lesson. Next time I break my bones on the rock

171

face, I'll remember this and choose differently.

"Mr Koven? Is there something I can fetch for you?"

One of my many housekeepers smooths her manicured hands over her dress, her painted face betraying no hint of alarm that I've burst in on her in the library. No hint, except the thrum of her pulse in her throat.

What's her name again?

God. This is awkward. I should remember my own staff. But I'm so rarely at home, I'd have more chance of recognizing a stranger in the street.

"No," I tell her, voice hoarse from the way my throat has clenched tight with frustration. Two whole weeks of being trapped at home—and I'm going mad after only three days. "No, thank you. I came to find a book."

Despite the natural stillness of reading, I'm a lifelong book-worm. I always have been. So this will be my saving grace over the next weeks—a chance to work through my rather ridiculous collection. There are first editions and rare books in this mansion that I've never even cracked open, to my great shame.

The housekeeper nods and plasters a smile over her face, then turns and marches swiftly for the doorway. Whatever she was doing in here, I suppose she won't continue while I'm near.

It's probably a manners thing. Something they learn in housekeeper school.

So why does that make me feel so damn lonely?

My library is a cavernous room, lined with floor to ceiling shelves crammed with book spines. A large desk worthy of a war general stands beside sparkling glass windows, prepped with a fountain pen and sheets of paper but—to my knowledge—never written on. I do all my own work at the much smaller desk in my office, safely away from distractions, and besides—the desk looks like an antique. I'd rather not scratch a piece of history.

A ladder leans against one of the bookshelves, taunting me and my busted hand, and a slew of squashy armchairs and reading tables are scattered through the room. The air is thick with the smell of paper and varnished wood. Why have I barely stepped foot in this room?

I suppose I've barely stepped foot in *most* of my rooms, always preferring to be outside. This mansion is wasted on me.

My footsteps echo over the floorboards as I stroll to the nearest shelf. I came here looking for a book, any book, but now that I'm here, the choice is almost overwhelming. I pluck the nearest hardback from the shelf with my good hand, flipping it over to read the cover.

Atomic Computing: the Implications.

Rolling my eyes, I slide it back on the shelf.

"Not a page turner?"

I jerk around at the voice. A maid stands in the doorway, a feather duster in one hand and an amused smile curling her mouth. She's wearing the normal uniform—a black tunic over dark pants, but something about the way she wears it is downright irreverent. Like she's just strolled off a catwalk, not come in here to clean.

When she shifts against the doorway, I notice the cast on her arm. It's larger than mine, and more crudely done.

I unstick my jaw.

"I've read it before."

She chuckles, running the feather duster over her tunic

absentmindedly. I watch the motion, transfixed. Her nails are clean cut but unpainted on the handle, her hands pale and slender.

"I'm more of an eReader kind of girl."

"And what do you read on your eReader?"

She smirks, the expression sending a bolt of heat down my spine.

"Wouldn't you like to know?"

Yes. God, yes. Desperately. I consider *ordering* her to tell me. She's my employee, is she not? But something tells me throwing my weight around this girl won't bring me answers—only her censure.

I don't want her censure. I want her silky red hair wrapped around my cock. I want to sink my thumb into the wet heat of her mouth, and I want her to moan around my knuckle.

Fuck. Who is this girl? I peer at her, mind racing as I try to put a face to the name. I glance over the resume and background check of every member of staff in this mansion; surely I'd remember a face like hers.

I snap my fingers. "Coral! You're Coral Walsh." Never have I been so pleased with my memory.

Just like that, the maid frosts over. The warm openness fades away, and she draws herself up. Her posture stiffens, and her smile turns polite.

"That's right, Mr. Koven."

"Call me Eli."

She tilts her head. "Do the other maids call you that?"

"No." I've barely exchanged two words with the other maids.

"Then I'd rather not, thank you, sir."

Her words are polite but cold, and I don't understand. Where has the teasing warmth of a few seconds ago gone? I frown at her, but she nods at me, unbowed, and crosses to the desk where she drifts the duster over the polished wood.

I clear my throat.

"What happened to your hand?"

She glances over at me, eyes quick, then looks back at her work.

"A cyclist came onto the sidewalk. And you?"

I look down at the plaster cast and snowy white bandages on my left hand. With her in the room, I'd almost forgotten its dull ache.

"A rock climbing accident."

Coral hums, smile wicked. "Self inflicted, then."

Yes. She's back with me.

"Guilty, your honor."

"Do you often bash yourself against rocks?" The teasing lilt to her voice has returned, and I can't help myself. I wander closer, eager to be near her. As near as she'll allow.

"At least once a day. Twice on Sundays."

"Ah." She nods sagely. "So it's not for fun. You're repenting your sins."

I actually consider that for all of a moment before I dismiss it as a joke. I don't climb to repent; I climb for the thrill. Everything I do—my work, my hobbies, my life—comes down to seeking that electric crackle of excitement.

That's why I build the best tech. Drive the fastest cars. Jump out of planes and eat the spiciest food I can order.

"It's true. I am a sinner down to my bones."

She bites her lip as she looks down, plump mouth curled in a faint smile, her uninjured arm sweeping over the surface of the desk. It must be the least dusty surface in all existence by now, but neither of us are in a hurry to move.

A thought occurs to me, and I stiffen.

"Do you always work when you're hurt? I know for a fact that I offer paid sick leave." My voice has come out too harsh, too clipped, and I know I've gone wrong again when she straightens up.

"Very good of you," Coral murmurs, turning away and wandering to the windows. "But I'm not sick. I can clean just fine."

"Not with both hands." I'm not making this better, but I can't seem to stop myself once I settle into an argument. "If you needed to lift something, or move a piece of furniture, you'd have to call someone away from their own work."

I don't care about that. So why do I feel the need to win this? To win everything, even as her pretty face clouds over and her eyes narrow at me over her shoulder. She sweeps the corners of the window panes, searching for non-existent cobwebs.

"I'll be sure not to disturb the other staff members, *sir*."

I clench my jaw, but keep going. God help me, I keep on pushing.

"Don't you see how that's more selfish than calling in sick? Everyone else will have to pick up your slack."

Her heels smack against the floorboards as she rocks down from her toes. And even though I'm her boss, even though I could fire her in a second, Coral Walsh strides from the room without another word. Her dismissal is clear, her reproach echoing in the silence, and I clench my uninjured fist as I watch her leave.

Fuck.

I could fire her.

But I'd never be able to look at myself in the mirror again. Not when, by the churning in my gut, I know I'm in the wrong.

And besides—if I fired her, there would never be any hope of stumbling upon her in my library again.

Instead, I suck in a deep breath, counting to five before gusting it out.

This was not an argument worth having. And now the first distraction I've had since my fall is gone.

I rub my clenched fist over my sternum.

Well, she can run. But this is my house.

Coral Walsh can't hide from me.

Billie

Coral's billionaire boss is… kind of a dick.

A hot one, but still. The guy's wound so tight, so bursting with frustrated energy, he's spoiling for a fight. Any fight.

I won't give him one.

I might want to—god, I want to take him on. The thought makes my skin flush hot. But I won't, not while impersonating my sister. She needs this job. Hell, *we* need her to have this job, and besides, she likes it. I won't ruin it for her.

Not while she's out there today, facing her worst nightmare for my modeling career. I chew on my lip as I wander through the mansion halls, wondering how it's going for her. Whether Archer Westbrook will give her a hard time.

I picture him scowling at her, making my sweet sister cry, and nerves pinch in my chest. God, what if I've hurt her? What if I've asked too much?

"There you are." A steel-hired woman with pursed pink lips emerges from a doorway, taking me by the elbow and steering me down a different corridor. "You're down for the pool house,

Coral. Can you manage with your hand?"

Mr. Koven's words float through my mind.

"I can manage," I say, mouth sour.

Even if I have to hold a mop with my teeth, I will manage.

The housekeeper drifts away, bustling off to corral the other maids, and I peer through the nearest doorways. Look up and down the corridor.

Where would a person hide a swimming pool?

"Need some help?"

His deep voice makes my heart skitter. I turn to face him, leaning in yet another doorway, his long legs stretching on forever in his faded jeans. His dark hair is messy, curling under his ears, and his pale gray eyes sparkle with amusement. He doesn't *look* like a billionaire, but then I suppose he's on sick leave.

Maybe that's why he's so bitter. I'm working with a busted arm while he's not.

"No, thank you." I pick a direction at random, plunging down a hallway. I don't need to look back to know that Mr. Koven follows me, his strides languid.

"The pool is the other way."

Shit. My footsteps slow to a halt. I clear my throat.

"It's a big house. I get lost sometimes."

"Naturally." The master of the mansion doesn't look suspicious when he stops at my side. If anything, he seems amused. Eager for another spat. He offers me the crook of his arm, his muscles bulging beneath his black long-sleeved shirt. "Allow me to escort you."

I eye him doubtfully.

He smiles and shrugs, the picture of innocence.

"Why do I feel like I'm cuddling up to a pit viper?" I tuck my good hand in his elbow. He tosses his head back and laughs, delighted, the rich sound bouncing off the walls. God, this mansion is so *quiet*. No wonder he's clearly gone mad.

"What a terrible way to speak of your boss."

I roll my eyes, not worried. The warm, teasing note is back in his voice. It affects me more than I'd like to admit. And the hard muscles under my fingertips, the clean, masculine scent drifting off him… I swallow.

"Lead the way, Mr. Koven."

The mansion is a rabbit warren. I don't know how Coral finds her way around. I half expect a Minotaur to burst out of a drawing room, we go through so many winding corridors. Coral's boss peppers me with questions as we walk, asking about my life, my hobbies, my dreams. I try my best to answer for Coral, giving the answers that might be hers, but I can feel the frustration mounting in the man at my side.

"Why are you lying?" he spits at last, yanking us to a stop. "You clearly do not just sit at home and bake."

I tear my hand away. "How the hell would you know?"

He levels me a *look*.

"These are not a baker's muscles." He squeezes my bare upper arm. "These are not a homebody's tan lines." He tugs my collar an inch to the side. The pale stripe of my bikini tie glows against my collarbone. I blink at him, lips parted, as he runs his analytical eye over my body. He catalogues everything: my toned muscles, the sun-kissed tint to my skin, the old mountain biking scar on my elbow.

He lays me bare with a single glance.

I shove away from him, stumbling back, and for a split second I think I see regret in his eyes. Then his face shutters, and he crosses his arms over his broad chest. Those shoulders—they're definitely the kind of shoulders that can scale cliffs.

"I don't tolerate liars on my staff, Coral."

"Miss Walsh," I hiss. His eyes darken.

"If you don't—"

"Don't what?" I give a harsh laugh. "Tell you about my private life? Reread your employment contracts, Mr. Koven. You have no right to these questions."

Forget the stupid pool. I wheel around and stalk away, back rigid and arms stiff at my sides.

I'll find it my own damn self.

Eli

I messed up. Again. Something about this maid makes me snappish and slow. She twists me in knots, so desperate for tiny details of her that I try to blunder my way to them by brute force.

She was right to smack me down. I would never demand details of my other employees like that, and yet with her, if I don't find out more about her, I'll go insane. Something about her heats my blood, makes the back of my neck prickle and my chest constrict. The second her tunic whips around the corner, I miss her.

Fuck.

Did she always affect me like this? Surely I've seen her before around my home. Yet I've never hungered for her this way before.

She's going entirely the wrong way to reach the pool, but something tells me Coral is in no mood to clean.

Fine. Let her storm around the mansion. Hopefully she'll burn off her anger and let me near again.

I scowl down at my cast, picking at the bandages as I stroll along the corridor to a set of French doors. This was a requirement for the architect—I wanted constant access to the outdoors. In every room, in every direction, the mansion has balconies, gardens, arched doorways. All for this: the salty breeze from the ocean tugging at my hair as I stroll down the stone steps into the grounds.

The breeze is cool, but still my face is flushed hot. Not just my face—I'm burning all over. I have been since that first glimpse of Coral in the library, tracing the feather duster over her stomach. Since I heard her husky voice, laced with amusement.

I hiss out a breath, adjusting my jeans. Two weeks of 'bed rest' of knowing she's near the whole time...

I'm screwed. She'll ruin me.

My assistant answers on the first ring. I press the phone to my ear, glancing back toward the mansion, but there's no movement through the French doors.

"David? I need everything we know about Coral Walsh. Email it over in the next ten minutes."

"Yes, sir. Is she a competitor?"

"What? No. She's a maid."

The silence is deafening. I scuff my sneaker over the patio. Then: "A maid, sir? At your residence?"

"Obviously." I scrub a hand over my face. "Where else would I have seen her?"

"Right. Uh. Okay. Is she—is there a problem with her work?"

Lord save me from pointless questions. I screw my eyes shut, breathing in a lungful of sea air.

"There's no problem. And David?"

"Yes?"

"Is this really how you want to spend your ten minutes?"

He apologizes and hangs up quickly, but I barely hear him at all. Not when I've just spotted a flash of red hair. Sure, plenty of people are redheads, but her glossy waves are something else. She looks like a mermaid.

I squint at the shadows moving in the next wing over. She found the pool.

Maybe she's had enough time to cool off. I shove my uninjured hand in my pocket and stroll across the grounds.

* * *

"Hi there, I'm just—oh. It's you."

The mop dangles by her side, and she sweeps her hair off her forehead with her cast. Her cheeks are pink from the pool house heat, and her forehead is dewy.

She's delicious.

"I missed you too, Coral."

"It's Miss Walsh," she grits out. She spins on her heel, turning her back to me and swabbing awkwardly at the tiles. I can't pretend that I'm an expert in mopping—not many tech moguls are—but I stride over and pluck the handle out of her hands.

"Hey!"

I offer it back. "Oh, I'm sorry. Did you want to do this part yourself?"

Her mouth twitches, and I fight back a grin. If I can make her laugh, *really* laugh, I'll die happy. And when she raises her chin, fixing those emerald green eyes on me in challenge, my cock hardens in my jeans.

"No. No, you're right. I'd like nothing more than to watch you try to mop, Mr. Koven."

"Have you no faith in me? I'm wounded."

She smirks. "None at all."

Coral hasn't stepped away. She's close enough that I could reach out and touch. I could rake my fingers through her red hair; I could run my thumb over her plump bottom lip. She watches me wide-eyed, breath hitching in her lungs.

Instead, I swab at the tiles, inhaling deeply through my nose, but the pool chemicals are too strong. I can't smell *her*, can't get a hint of her shampoo or perfume.

It's another thing to add to the list. Another detail I desperately need.

"Why pay your staff if you'd rather do it all yourself?"

I grin at her. "For the company, I suppose."

I'm joking of course, but I'm surprised to hear a ring of truth to my words. I have plenty of friends, an army's worth of employees, but since exchanging a few words with Coral in the library, I've felt oddly lonely whenever she's out of my sight.

This is a big mansion to live in alone. It never bothered me before.

Now I don't want her to leave.

Not even to go home at the end of her shift. I want her to finish work, change out of her tunic, and stay with me. Laughing and teasing and undressing me with her eyes the way she does when she thinks I'm not looking.

Wait. Scratch that. I don't want her to work a shift then stick around. I don't want her to work here at all.

I want her to live here. To eat breakfast at the kitchen bar; to slip into this pool in a skimpy bikini.

I want her in my bed. On my balcony. Perched on my lap in my office.

God. What is happening to me?

"Mr. Koven?"

Coral frowns at me, concerned. Apparently I've been staring at her in wide-eyed horror. I clear my throat, rubbing my cast over my chest, and swab harder at the tiles.

"Call me Eli. Do you like working here, Coral?"

Is it just me, or does she shrink inside herself when I call her that? Does she honestly prefer being called Miss Walsh?

She nods, plucking at her tunic.

"Yes. Very much."

"And did you... always... want to be a maid?"

Shit, what a weird question to ask. And I said it so awkwardly, she'll think I'm insulting her. I'm not judging her—far from it. I fully believe that this young woman could be anything she chose. The world must offer itself up to her.

She snorts, amused, and my shoulders relax. I swab a new section, relishing the ache in my muscles. It's been too long already since I moved my body.

"I, um." She darts a glance at me, chewing on her lip. Deciding how much she wants to reveal.

All of it, I will her privately. I want all of it. Every thought in her head, every secret dream, every whisper-soft inch of her skin.

"I want to be a model, actually."

"Ah." I laugh bitterly. "You won't be here long."

Her frown deepens. "What do you mean?"

I wave vaguely up and down the length of her body with my cast.

"I give it a week, max, before the whole world knows your name."

Her cheeks flush with pleasure and she ducks her head. Not

186

out of shyness, but to keep her reaction to herself. She's private, then. And when she looks up again, that spark from earlier is back. The tension crackles in the air between us.

Her eyes dip to my throat. Down to my chest, sliding over my broad shoulders. Coral likes what she sees when she takes in my body. She's shameless in her perusal, her gaze greedy as she wets her lip.

I swell harder in my jeans, and her eyes drop there, too.

Fuck.

"Do you enjoy torturing me, Miss Walsh?"

Her mouth twitches. "Am I torturing you? How?"

"By looking at me like something to eat." I drop the mop handle with a clatter, stepping close, but she doesn't retreat an inch. She looks up at me, pupils blown wide. "Do you want a taste, darling?" Her chest shudders under her tunic as she sucks in a breath. "Shall I push you to your pretty knees?"

My heart stops when she leans forward. Coral places a palm on my chest, rocking up onto her toes to bring her face close to mine. I'm rigid with tension, practically vibrating with the effort to hold myself back. To keep from crushing her against my chest and *claiming* her.

She smirks, then runs the tip of her pert nose up the side of my throat. There's a flash of white, then she's pulling my bottom lip between her teeth.

A groan shudders through me, and she lets me go and steps back.

"Maybe you should. Do you think you could handle it, Mr. Koven?"

Holy shit. I've never been so hard. And judging by the smug look on her face, she knows it too. She sashays over to the fallen mop, bending at the waist to pluck it off the tiles.

Billie

A breath hisses between my teeth when he grips my hips, tugging my ass back against him. Coral's boss is hard as steel, the length of him nestled between my ass cheeks, and triumph surges through me as I straighten and lean back against his chest.

We're both breathing hard, the sounds harsh in the pool house where the only other noise is the gentle slosh of turquoise water against the pool walls.

I shouldn't have baited him. Shouldn't have pushed him to this.

But I can't pretend to be sorry.

I squirm my hips, trying to feel him better, and let my head drop back onto his shoulder. Mr. Koven—Eli—scrapes his teeth over my bared throat, nipping at the vulnerable skin.

A hook twists in my lower abdomen. A pulse thrums between my legs, ticking like a time-bomb.

"Are you always such a fucking tease, Coral?"

I wilt in his arms. Hearing my sister's name as he rocks

against my ass—yeah, that's a downer.

"Miss Walsh," I whisper. I don't care if it makes me sound like some Victorian dominatrix. I don't want him calling me by the wrong name.

Eli pauses. My heart begins to sink, but then he winds his uninjured hand through my hair. He grabs a fistful of my waves, tugging my head back with just enough force to make me gasp.

Heat floods my pussy. I whimper, squeezing my thighs together.

"You haven't answered my question. Are you always such a tease, Miss Walsh?"

It's ridiculous, but the fact that he's willing to call me that warms my insides. Makes me go all gooey. Because now I can pretend this is really between *us*—Eli and Billie. Not Eli and my sister.

"No," I tell him, and it's the truth. "I guess you bring out the worst in me."

His chuckle is dark. Smoky.

"The worst? Oh, I hope so."

His tongue lathes me from collarbone to earlobe. It's like he wants to consume me, to swallow me whole, and god help me but I want that too. Shivers race across my skin and I melt back against him, pliant and all his.

"And you? Do you always lick your maids?"

Because I need to know. Is this as special as it feels?

This time, his laugh is short and humorless.

"Hardly." Then he brightens. "Why? Are you jealous, Miss Walsh?"

Yes. The thought of Eli doing this with another maid, even another *woman*, makes me want to spit with envy. Makes me want to trash the pool house and set fire to the grounds.

I won't, obviously. I'm not insane. But I do rock back against him harder.

Eli sucks in a pleased breath. "So you *are* jealous."

"No."

"You are, baby. You're two seconds from tearing my shirt down the middle and rubbing your scent on my skin."

"You wish," I grind out, though the image makes me flush hotter. He's right, I *do* want to tear his clothes. To mess up his hair and scratch his chest so hard I draw blood. Partly to wipe that cocky smile off his face, and partly to show everyone else he's *mine*.

"Shall I tell you a secret?" He nips at my earlobe, rubbing strands of my hair between his finger and thumb. "I'm jealous too. I want to suck bruises all over your creamy skin just so everyone knows you're taken."

"I am?"

"*Yes.*"

I scoff, but it sounds weak. "I don't remember agreeing to that."

A hand presses at my lower back, arching me away even as he pulls my head harder back. I'm bent in the most shameless position, my ass squirming against his cock as my spine bows and my chest thrusts at the ceiling.

Eli saws his cock between my ass cheeks, up and down, and the size of him makes my mouth water even through our layers of clothes.

"Think about it, darling." He bites my shoulder, then soothes it with a lick. "If you want this cock, you'll have to be mine."

It should be ridiculous. A laughable statement. But right this second, I'd give my left arm to feel his rock-hard length slide inside me. If he's this domineering, this possessive when our clothes are still on, when we haven't even kissed yet...

I whimper.

"Leave the mop." Eli steps away, letting go of me suddenly, and I stagger, my knees like jelly. "I need your services elsewhere."

I wheel around, cheeks hot. "My *services*—"

"Your feather duster." He grins, eyes twinkling. "My office. Now."

Usually, I hate being bossed around. It's the worst thing about fashion shoots—grumpy men barking orders.

But when Eli does it, my pussy clenches and my clit throbs. God, what is happening to me?

Who is this girl who whimpers and writhes against a strange man in a pool house? Whose thoughts scatter to the wind every time he murmurs in her ear?

I don't know, but I want to find out. I stumble forward and follow Eli into the grounds.

* * *

Cleaning should not be a sexy activity.

I know *that* for sure.

It's something you do because you have to, to not be a slob, and maybe there's a flash of satisfaction for a job well done.

Coral *likes* cleaning. It's one of the many ways we are completely different, never mind that our faces are identical. She says she finds it therapeutic—the methodical way you work around a room, finding a rhythm, letting your mind drift and your muscles burn.

She likes the quiet, too, and the mansion's views.

Me, I find the quiet here eerie. Kind of sad, like loneliness echoes through the halls. But the views… I glance over at Eli, leaning back against his desk as he watches me dust with dark eyes.

Yeah. The views are pretty freaking fantastic.

His dark hair is even more rumpled since our messy clasp in the pool house. His eyes shine beneath his lowered brows, and his firm jaw is clenched tight. The hand with the cast rests in his lap, the fingertips still and curled over the plaster, but his other hand grips the edge of the desk so hard his knuckles are white. Like he's clinging on for dear life to keep from lunging toward me.

A long-sleeved black cotton shirt stretches over his chest and shoulders, hiding all the ridges and planes of muscle that I felt against my back. His gray jeans are soft and faded, clinging to his toned thighs, and god, I want to scratch my fingernails down those jeans. I want to pop the button open with my teeth.

"What are you thinking?" he murmurs, cocking his head as I run my feather duster along his office bookshelves. I keep sneaking glances at him, tiny snatches which make my body thrum. "I can't tell if you're angry or so turned on you might snap."

I choke out a laugh, rocking onto my toes to reach for the top shelf. My tunic rises, brushing against the backs of my thighs, and I suddenly wish I didn't have leggings on.

"The second one."

He growls in approval. The low, rumbling noise stiffens my nipples under Coral's tunic.

"Are you ready for me to fix that for you?"

I chew on my lip, thinking. Eli made it very clear—if I want his cock, first I must agree to be *his*.

I can't do that. He thinks I'm Coral. He doesn't even know my real name.

I shake my head, hair drifting over my shoulders, but my voice is hollow when I speak.

"No. I can't agree to your terms."

"Why not?" Eli sounds ready to tear the desk apart with his bare hands, injury be damned. "Is there..." His voice drops. "Is there someone else?"

"No." I glare at him over my shoulder. "I'm not a cheater. How awful do you think I am?"

I'm pissed off, but even so, my words settle him. He sinks back against the desk, relaxed again.

Eli's office is like a smaller version of the library, but with a balcony that stretches the whole length of it. He keeps the French doors open, the breeze rolling in off the sea, and all the papers on his desk flutter beneath their paperweights. A few potted plants bring pops of green, their waxy leaves waving in the breeze.

It's a nice room. Very... him. A mix of modern and classic with the wild edge of nature thrown in. Eli Koven is a man with teeth and claws.

"I have money," he says mildly. "More money than a person could spend."

I breathe in hard through my nose and count to ten. When I spin to face him, the feather duster gripped in one hand, I force myself to speak evenly.

"Why do you mention that, Eli?" I hold up a palm when he starts to talk. "Because you should think very carefully about your next words. If you're about to imply that I can be bought, that I'm some kind of gold digger, then I swear I will stick this feather duster so deep up your ass it will tickle your brain."

He throws back his head and roars with laughter. My mouth twitches, but I press it into a firm line and wait for his answer.

I don't care if he's hot. If his laugh is infectious.

If *that's* what he thinks of me, I won't spend another minute in his presence.

"God. No." He scrubs a hand over his jaw, still chuckling. "That's not what I meant to imply."

"Then what did you—"

He shrugs. "I merely wanted to show that if there are other difficulties keeping you away, I could help you with them."

Jeez. I see now why tech guys are stereotyped as awkward.

"Why didn't you just say *that*?"

He grins, cheeks dimpling.

"Your eyes flash bright green when you're mad."

"You... I..." My mouth opens and shuts. I stand here like an outraged goldfish, staring at this gorgeous, infuriating man. And when he pushes to his feet, strolling across his office, I back up to the bookshelves until they press against my shoulder blades.

"Running away?" His gaze rakes over me. "Tell me to stop, Miss Walsh. Tell me to leave you alone, and I promise I'll walk out that door."

I swallow hard... and say nothing. Triumph lights his eyes.

Eli comes closer and closer until his chest is inches from mine. Until I can feel the heat of his body; until his breath stirs the flyaway strands of my hair. He's so close, so freaking close, that if I arched my back like earlier, my stiff nipples would brush against him through my tunic.

"What shampoo do you use?" he asks suddenly. "What scent?" He ducks his head and breathes me in at the base of my neck. He lifts a red lock of my hair, pressing it to his nose and sniffing it too, then shakes his head, annoyed. "You smell like the swimming pool. I can't tell."

Is he really so eager to know?

"Green apple," I murmur.

"Green apple," he repeats, muttering to himself. "Yes. That fits."

I nudge his knee with mine. "You're kind of weird."

He steps closer, flattening me against the bookshelves. His palms skate up the sides of my waist—cupping and squeezing on one side, and the steady slide of his cast on the other.

"Not weird. Just infatuated."

"Already?" I rasp. "You've only known me one day."

He frowns down at me, and I could kick myself. Of course he's known Coral for more than a day, and I've blown it, screwed this up, but then he shakes his head.

"It doesn't matter. I knew the second I saw you."

"Knew what?" I gasp. His thumb skates over my nipple, and I arch my back, pressing harder into his hand.

Eli hums and sniffs the crown of my head.

"That I had to have you," he says simply. My head is swimming from his touch, from his words, from his manly scent—like ocean air and pine needles. Maybe that's why I do it: lose all my good sense. Push away from the bookshelves, nudge him back, and drop to my knees.

"Fuck. Look at you." Eli crowds back immediately, cradling my cheek in his hand. "Do you want to suck my cock, darling?"

I nod, reaching up with greedy hands. My bruised fingers are clumsy inside the cast, and I curse as I fumble with the button of his jeans.

"Let me help—"

I smack his hand away, rock forward, and tug it open with my teeth.

"Yes," Eli hisses in approval as I draw his cock free. It's thick and so hard it must surely be painful, yet the skin is soft and warm under my grip. I give an experimental tug, toes curling beneath me when he groans.

"Say please." I smirk up at him, and he grins back, eyes feral and dancing. This man is a loose cannon, wild and unpredictable, but I want nothing more than to push him to the edge.

"Please," he grits out through clenched teeth. "Fuck. Coral. Suck me, baby."

"Miss Walsh." I squeeze him once, hard, in warning, and he rocks into my grip. But when I glare up at him, he nods and pets my hair.

"Miss Walsh. Suck me down, darling."

I'm more than happy to obey.

I settle back on my heels and regard the monster in front of me. It's bigger than I realized back in the pool house, and it made my breath catch then. But it's not the length that makes my pussy clench—it's the breadth. When I wrap my hand around him, my fingers and thumb don't meet.

My first lick is catlike. Teasing, just like him. I taste the salty bead of fluid gathered at the tip, moaning and gazing up at him with wide eyes.

He curses and thrusts his hips, his cock sliding through my grip.

"So impatient," I murmur.

Eli narrows his eyes.

That's all the warning I get before he grips my chin and pulls it open, pushing his cock into my mouth. A thrill shudders through me at being used like this—having my mouth invaded for his pleasure. It's like everything else in the world fades away except for the heavy weight of him on my tongue; the stretch of my lips; the slurping noises that I'd never thought I'd make.

But I make them, and much more, moaning greedily and whimpering, swirling my tongue over his cock as he cradles my head in place and thrusts so deep he hits the back of my throat.

"Fuck. Yeah. Do you like that, baby?"

I moan louder, nodding and squirming on the floor. I wedge one heel under my pussy, grinding down on it and rubbing my clit until the pressure starts to build.

Eli stares down at me, eyes glassy, then they suddenly widen. His expression heats, and he fucks my face harder.

"I can see what you're doing, baby. Getting yourself off. Humping your own foot because you're so needy to come."

His words are fuel tossed on the fire, and the crackling embers in my core burst into twenty-foot flames. I cry out, rocking harder, slurping him deeper, and his fingers tighten on my jaw until they're just this side of pain.

The thought of bruises—of shadowed fingerprints where anyone could see and guess what we've been doing—it stops my breath. I freeze, muscles rigid, a cry tearing from my mouth as waves of pleasure ripple from my core. It scorches through my body, lighting my nerve ends on fire, and when I finally slump back on my heels, my ears are ringing.

Eli draws his cock from my mouth with a pop, cursing and working himself with his own hand, before warm stripes of his come paint my cheeks.

I grin up at him, chest heaving and eyes wet, a flushed, sticky mess.

I've never felt so freaking alive.

"Good girl," he grinds out, his deep voice like gravel, and my pussy throbs in response. He tucks my hair behind my ear. "Good girl."

I stay kneeling as he crosses to the desk, rummaging in the drawers before he comes back and crouches in front of me. He wipes my face so tenderly, his touch so gentle on my raw lips, that my heart cracks open.

Shit. I wish he really were mine.

And more than that—I want to be *his*. His lover. His pet. His plaything. It's such a cruel joke, to have him like this—to know how he tastes, how he feels. The way his eyes twinkle when he helps me up from the floor.

Because I can't have him. He thinks I'm my twin sister, and if I tell him the truth, he'll know I've lied to him since the first second I saw him.

I can't bear his rejection. For once in my life, I'll be a coward instead.

"I'd better go." He frowns at my hoarse words. "I, um. I have work to do."

"Cor—Miss Walsh." He catches himself at the last second, but the reminder is still there. This is my sister's job, my sister's *boss*, and I can't ruin it for her.

Not more than I already have.

"Goodbye, Eli." I step around him and leave the office, my chest caving in.

Eli

ᜒᜒᜒ

This can't be happening.

I can't have found the one woman for me, the one who lights up my soul, and watched her walk out the door on the same day. My heart thumps sickly inside my rib cage, and I stand frozen in the center of my office.

Lost. Confused. Still so turned on from her touch that my teeth ache.

I rub a hand over my jaw. Did I... hurt her? She seemed into it too, moaning and squirming, her cheeks flushed with arousal, but maybe I misread the signs.

God. If I hurt her...

I'll never forgive myself.

I was rough. I thrust deep into her mouth, until I hit the back of her throat. I acted by instinct the whole time, the two of us slipping into our roles like we were made for them, and I spoke crassly to her. Ground out sweet, filthy words that made her gasp.

But what if that was all in my head? My gut sinks as I replay what we just did—what *I* did to my maid.

What if she didn't want any of it? I lurch to the side, sickness roiling in my stomach. I need to find her—need to make sure she's okay. Need to apologize and do whatever it takes to make this right.

The office door bounces against the wall as I charge out into the corridor. The mansion is quiet, the silence echoing through the halls, slanted rectangles of sunshine spilling over the floorboards. I whip my head back and forth so fast my neck aches, but Coral is gone.

She's gone.

A man walks past the nearest doorway, dressed in the black tunic of the staff uniform. I charge forward, clenching the door frame in my uninjured hand until the wood creaks. He glances over, then jerks as he recognizes me, straightening and clasping his hands behind his back. He's young, can't be more than thirty, with dark hair and a sculpted face, and the thought of this man working near Coral...

Jealousy tears through my chest.

I force it down. Ignore it. I'm a man, not an animal, and I won't mistreat another member of my staff. But still, I have to spit my question between gritted teeth.

"Coral Walsh. Have you seen her?"

The man blinks at me, eyes darting away and back.

"Um. I'm sorry. Who?"

Forget it. I wrench myself off the door frame, charging down the corridor like a mad man. A roaring sound fills my ears, my eyes fuzzy with fear, and I let instinct guide me through the winding halls of my home. Every step, every aching beat of my heart, is another time I think her name.

Coral. Coral.

Where is she?

My feet lead me down a sunlit corridor, and the scent of chlorine lingers in the air. My footsteps quicken, suddenly sure, and when I push through the entrance into the pool house, there she is.

My mermaid.

Sitting on a lounger, her hands upturned in her lap, staring at the turquoise pool in a daze. She glances up when I burst in, and a frown creases her forehead, but she doesn't move or say anything. Like she's in a dream.

"Miss Walsh," I grit out, and she jerks, eyes widening. Like she's finally realized I'm real. She looks around desperately for an exit, but I'm already striding across to her. More than anything, I want to scoop her up in my arms, to crush her against my chest and tell her she's mine.

I won't overstep again. I stop in front of her lounger, sinking to my knees on the warm tiles.

"I'm sorry," I rasp. "I'm so sorry. I never meant to hurt you." She blinks at me, confused.

"Eli? What—"

"In... In my office. I was rough with you." I suck in a deep breath, holding her emerald gaze. God, she's beautiful. "Please forgive me. It will never happen again. Whatever you need to feel safe and comfortable at work here, tell me. I'll put it in place."

Her cheeks pink from the memory of what we just did, but she shakes her head hard, her red hair drifting over her shoulders.

"It wasn't—you didn't hurt me." She bites her plump lip. "I liked it."

Relief surges through me, sweet and cool. I sit back on my

heels, almost lightheaded with it.

"Then why did you leave?"

She shrugs, and she looks so damn miserable, I can't resist. I reach out and smooth my cast over her hair. Stray locks wind around my bruised fingertips, silky and soft, and it's the best sensation I've ever felt. Better than any painkiller.

I wait, but she doesn't offer anything more. Just leans her head into my palm.

"If I'd known it was a one time thing..." I swallow hard at the thought. "That's not how I'd have wanted it to go."

"What would you change?" she whispers, eyes fixed on the hollow of my throat. I tip her chin up.

"I would have kissed you first."

There's plenty of time for her to move away. I make sure of it, still raw from the fears which consumed me in my office. The thought of touching this woman in any way she dislikes—every molecule of my body revolts.

So I lean in, achingly slow, the pool house silent except for the rasp of our shared breaths. And I stop when my mouth is a hair's breadth from hers.

"I won't kiss you unless you ask me to."

She huffs out a breath, lips parting, but she doesn't ask like I expect. Doesn't push me away either. No—she surges forward, her mouth sealing against mine. With her hand fisted in my shirt and her tongue licking into my mouth, Coral Walsh kisses the last sane thoughts out of my brain.

I groan, hands sliding into her hair, crowding closer until I kneel between her legs. She parts her thighs easily, shuffling to the edge of the lounger until we're sealed together tight. She's so warm, burning bright against every inch of my front, and I'm hard again, pressed against her core. We cling and kiss and sway together, like addicts jonesing for each other's touch after just a few minutes apart.

"Baby." I tear my mouth away, kissing along her jaw. When I suck a bruise onto that pretty throat, she sighs into my ear. "Baby, I need you."

She's nodding, scrabbling at the button on my jeans, but that's not what I mean.

What I *mean* is that if I'd known she'd only want me once, *I'd* have been the one on my knees. The one tasting and teasing; the one made vulnerable.

If this is my last chance, I'm taking it.

And I'm putting my mouth on this woman.

She sucks in a surprised breath when I hook my fingers in her leggings, but she lifts her hips and helps me shuffle them down. She watches my hands smooth over her thighs with glassy eyes, and her breaths already come fast as I push her legs further apart.

"Are you..." She wets her lip, still half dazed. "Are you sure?"

My rough laugh echoes through the pool house.

"I'm sure."

I sit back on my heels, soaking in the full view of her. The wild tangle of her hair; her rumpled tunic hiked up around her waist; the lilac triangle of her panties.

The damp spot on the front of the fabric.

Fuck. That damp spot.

I lunge forward and she squeaks in surprise, the sound melting into a moan as I rub my face over the lace. I mouth at the fabric, licking her through her panties, and Coral curses softly and winds her fingers through my hair.

"Now who's a tease?" she murmurs, and I smile against her covered pussy. Turning my head, I press kisses to the sensitive insides of her thighs, licking and nibbling around the edges of her panties but never dipping inside. *"Eli."* she tugs my hair and I laugh, the sound vibrating over her skin.

Without warning, I slide her panties to the side and lathe my tongue up her pussy. She's hot and slick and perfect, swollen with want, her salty, tangy taste the best thing I've ever had on my tongue. I bury my face between her thighs like a starving man at his last meal, licking deep into her center and drawing up to suckle on her clit.

"Eli!" Her thighs snap closed around my head, clamping me in place—as if I'd ever try to escape. As if there is any goddamn place on the planet I'd rather be.

"So fucking good," I tell her, the words vibrating through her slick folds. "So fucking delicious, baby."

She moans, her hips rocking against my tongue, and I growl in approval as she pushes me harder against her core. This is us—what I sensed instinctively in my office. We're both rough with each other, desperate and wild in our need to get closer, closer, closer.

I love it as much as she did.

I want to fucking drown in this girl.

When I slide my middle finger inside her, she clamps down, her muscles rippling against me. The thought of that on my cock makes me groan, and I pump deeper, crooking my finger and rubbing against that secret spot.

Her thighs lock beside my ears, muscles shuddering, and the *sound* she makes.

It's part groan. Part sigh. And she says my name like a prayer.

I keep licking her through her orgasm, keep pumping my finger into the tight clasp of her pussy. I don't stop until she slumps on the pool lounger, her thighs falling away from my ears. And when I sit back on my heels, chest heaving and chin slick and shining with the evidence, I don't wipe it off. I'm not ready to have her gone from my skin.

"Come here," she murmurs, tugging me forward by my shirt. She wipes my face with the hem of her tunic, her hands gentle against my jaw. The rough scrape of her cast on one side, and her warm skin on the other—I close my eyes and draw in a shuddering breath.

"It's my turn to apologize."

I blink my eyes open. Coral's smile is rueful.

"What for?"

She shrugs, feigning casualness. "For grabbing you like that. Rubbing—rubbing myself on you." Her cheeks flush darker. "I'm sorry."

"Don't," I grit out. "Don't say that. I fucking loved it, baby. I want you to use me like that every day for the rest of our lives."

A light dies behind her eyes at my words. And I know it's intense, wanting her so badly after just one day, but surely I can't be alone in this? At every moment, we've been matched in passion. Equally desperate for each other, orbiting each other like planets, and fuck, how have I misread this again?

"Coral…" She slumps further, and dread slides through my stomach. "Tell me you feel the same way."

"I'm sorry."

My breath saws in and out of my lungs. Her hands drop away from my shirt.

"It was…" She pauses. Steels herself. Then caves in my chest with only a few words. "It was just a bit of fun."

My ears ring as I sit back. As I push to my feet, staring down at her on the lounger like I've never seen her before.

A bit of fun.

"Fine," I rasp. Harsh words line up on my tongue, but I choke them back. "Alright." My sneakers echo on the tile as I move back a few steps. "I'll... Goodbye, Coral."

I stride out of the pool house before I can say anything else. Before I say something I regret, or push her too hard. It's her decision, and I'll respect it, but fuck—my heart throbs so hard I miss a breath.

I misread the situation. We want different things.

That's fine.

That's normal.

I've never even cared before.

So why do I feel like a part of me just died?

Billie

❧❧❧

Whoever said love hurts hit the nail on the freaking head. When Eli strides out of the pool house, my chest cracks open down the middle. I'm surprised I don't bleed out into a puddle on the floor.

Why *him?*

Why did it have to be Coral's boss? Why did I have to meet him while pretending to be my twin?

A cruel slideshow plays before my eyes: how things could have gone. How we might have met on any other day. There would have been no need for this pain, for all this rejection and crushed hope. I would have leaped into his arms and never let go.

I curl up in a ball, like if I crush my knees to my chest and wrap my arms tight, I can hold all the heartbreak inside. Sobs wrack my frame, and when the pool house door pushes open, I barely have the energy to lift my head.

"Coral!" It's the housekeeper from earlier. She hustles over to me, eyes wide with alarm. "Goodness, dear. Are you ill?"

"Yes," I sniff. Better to say that than to admit what I've really been doing. I've already caused such a mess for my sister—I won't add any more to that. "I have a terrible headache."

"Well go home!" The housekeeper helps me up and ushers me to the doorway. "Go home and rest, dear. We'll manage for the rest of your shift."

I barely cleaned for the beginning of it either, and right now I feel two inches tall. All I've done today is wreak havoc—I've messed around on the job, hooked up with the boss, and poor Coral will have to deal with the wreckage.

God. She'll hate me. Hot tears slide down my cheeks.

I'll make it up to her. I'll make things right. And first—I duck into the library on my way through the halls. I cross to the desk, digging through the drawers until I find a notepad and pen. Something meant for writing, not display, like the fancy fountain pen and sheaf of paper.

My note is short. A peace offering. No real explanation, but I hope it will make my sister's life easier.

Eli,

I'm so sorry about today. I wish more than anything that I could explain, but I can't. It's not only my secret to tell.

Please know that what happened between us meant a lot to me. And though it can never happen again, I won't forget it either.

Miss Walsh

I fold it up and address it to him, then ask a passing staff member to take it to the boss. I watch the man hurry away down the hall, my note gripped in his hand, then turn and make my way to the front door.

My wrist aches inside my cast, and the sun blinds me when I step onto the driveway. I walk quickly, my legs still wobbly from the way Eli made me come, arousal still clenched tight in my core.

Better. I'll do better. I'll make it up to Coral, and I'll never be so thoughtless again.

And hopefully, if I'm lucky, one day I'll think of Eli without wanting to cry.

* * *

When Coral comes through our apartment door, she looks how I feel. Sad and tired, her eyes red from crying, like we're two teddy bears with the stuffing knocked out of us.

We sit together quietly. Share the comfort that only sisters can bring, with soft breaths and closed eyes and murmured questions, our heads tipped back against the sofa. Evening sunshine slants through the windows, painting the apartment gold, and the potted plants wave in the gentle breeze.

And when we finally push up to cook dinner, to move on with this terrible day, at least we're doing it together.

Coral and I are a team. Always. No matter how hard things get.

Then the calls come.

We're clearing up dishes, bellies full of pasta, when Coral's phone starts to vibrate on the counter. We both ignore it, the kitchen filled with the gentle slosh of Coral's arms in the sink.

The phone stops. There's a beat of silence. Then it starts to buzz again.

Cold dread slides down my spine.

I snatch the phone up before Coral can see the screen, my sister gaping at my crazy behavior. But then my phone starts to buzz too, and she sprints for it faster than I've ever seen her move.

Crap.

Okay.

Okay.

Apparently we've both had… unusual days. And when it all comes out, with Coral knocking on my bedroom door, her face pale and my phone clutched in her hand, I choke back a manic laugh.

We've both fallen for each other's boss. Gotten mixed up with men who don't even know our real names. Maybe it's selfish, but a tiny part of me is glad that we're going through this together. That we've *both* made mistakes.

We agree: I'll go and meet Archer Westbrook in Coral's place and break their fling off. And Coral will call Eli and turn him down for me.

Neither of us can face it otherwise. And we can't tell these men about our lie. Not when they've already burrowed into our hearts.

It's a relief to have a plan, but I'm not proud as I grab my jacket and head out the door.

Poor Eli. He deserves so much more.

Eli

Coral Walsh is a liar.

At least, *this* one is. There seem to be two. At first, I think I must remember it wrong. She tucks her hair behind her ear with her left hand, and I frown at the screen of our video call. The imposter keeps talking, that familiar face solemn but her voice softer than before. She trips over some words, her cheeks flushing at her stutter.

Her *left* hand. She used her left. The hand that wore a cast. Something's not right.

A memory tickles the back of my brain. A red-headed maid with a stutter, quietly cleaning my office while I worked at the desk.

It's her. *This* is Coral Walsh. A woman I've seen many times before in my life, but who I've never spared a second thought for.

So who the hell did I lose my mind over? Who took my breath away the second I saw her?

Coral's still talking, gravely informing me that what happened between us was a mistake. Except I've never touched *this* woman. Does she think I'm a complete fool? Does she think I can't see the different way she holds herself, hear the different cadence to her voice?

"Miss Walsh," I interrupt. She blinks at me. "I expect you at work tomorrow morning."

I hang up without another word, tossing my phone onto my desk. I'm tired of all the lies. My hand aches inside my cast, a physical manifestation of my dark mood, and I tip back in my chair and drum my fingers on the wood.

A twin sister. Obviously. One who lives in the area—perhaps even with Coral. I pull up the email my assistant sent earlier with Coral Walsh's details. I scroll down to the address and stare at it with dry eyes.

Just a conversation. That's all I want. An explanation from the girl who turned me inside out. Then I'll leave her alone.

I check Coral's listed emergency contact, mouth twisting at the name written there, then push back my chair and stride out of the office.

* * *

I sit in the idling limousine, staring up at the apartment block. It's modest but charming, with plain features but plants, string lights, and colorful blinds in most of the windows. The people who live here may not be wealthy, but the stairs are swept clean and the squares of warm light in the windows make my chest ache with longing.

This apartment block puts my empty mansion to shame. I clench my jaw, staring up at the windows.

I'll go and knock in a moment. I'm gathering my thoughts;

trying to swallow back the anger of being lied to so that I don't scare her away.

Billie Blue Walsh.

The little liar who stole my heart.

"Sir?" the driver calls. "Shall I park up?"

I gust out a sigh. "No. Wait here." I won't be long. Billie made herself clear earlier: she wants nothing more to do with me. I just need to understand what the hell happened today, then I'll give her all the space she wants.

Even if it hollows me out. Even though I miss her so badly I can't breathe properly.

Warm evening air washes over me as I throw the door open, stepping out onto the sidewalk. I scowl up at the apartments, slamming the door shut behind me, and I've barely taken three steps when a voice freezes me in place.

"Eli?"

She's here. With a cast on her left wrist and a frown on her pretty face.

Billie.

She hovers on the sidewalk, her face pinched and pale. A light jacket covers her shoulders, but she still wraps her arms around her waist, squeezing like she needs the hug.

"Billie," I rasp, and she sucks in a sharp breath, stumbling back half a step.

"You—you know?"

"Yeah." The confirmation hits me square in the gut. "I know. I know that you came to work for your sister." I prowl closer. "I know that you *lied* to me all day. And then you made her do your dirty work and turn me down so you didn't have to."

I spit the last few words, I'm so fucking mad, and she flinches, gaze dropping to the ground. She looks so defeated, so sad, and I want to wrap her in my arms and rock her gently.

I push that urge away. She doesn't want that from me. So I'll get my answers and go.

"*Why?* Why did you lie to me, Billie? At first, I get it—you didn't want to get your sister in trouble. But after we kissed? After—after everything else? *Why?*"

"Because I'm a coward." Despite her words, her voice rings out loud and clear. She scrubs at her cheeks and I realize they're wet with her tears. *Fuck.* My hand twitches towards her, but I yank it back. Cross my arms over my chest so I won't touch where I'm not wanted. The breeze tugs on her red hair, strands floating out of a long braid, and it looks darker in the evening light.

"You're not a coward," I scoff. "You waltzed into my mansion like you owned it."

"That's different."

"How?"

"Because I didn't care then what you thought of me!" She throws her hands up, face etched with misery as she rants on. "Then when we—after everything that happened, I *knew* I should tell you who I really was. But the thought of your rejection, of-of seeing the exact face you're pulling now—"

She breaks off, glaring at the sidewalk. Her throat bobs as she swallows. And when she speaks again, her voice is calmer. Measured.

"I'm sorry, Eli. You're right to be angry. This whole day I've made nothing but bad decisions." She sighs and looks up again, raising her hands. "Please don't hold this against Coral. It was all my idea. All of it."

My pulse thumps in my ears. I'm too busy fixating on what she said a moment ago to reply.

My rejection. She couldn't face my rejection.

"Billie," I say slowly. "Get in the car."

"But—"

I yank the door open. "*In.*"

She scowls and stomps past me, ducking inside, but she can't hide the spots of color on her cheeks. Billie likes to be bossed around.

I remember. I remember it *all.*

"Take us home," I tell the driver, Billie darting a glance at me at those words. I ignore her and press the button to raise the partition. I wait until the divider is completely up and we've pulled away from the sidewalk before I turn to her.

She stares back at me, wide-eyed.

I frown. "Put your seat belt on." I never want to see a cast on her again.

Billie huffs but obeys. I reach over and wind an escaped lock of red hair around my finger. She watches, spellbound, her chest shuddering with each breath as I stroke the pad of my thumb over the glossy strands.

"You still want me," she whispers, almost to herself.

"*Always.*"

"Even though I lied to you?"

I smirk, but there's an edge to my words. "Don't do it again."

She shakes her head before I've finished talking.

"I won't. I swear. God, Eli…"

"Yes, Miss Walsh?"

She snorts and tips her head back, grinning up at the ceiling.

"You don't have to call me that anymore."

"Maybe I've got a taste for it."

"I just didn't want you saying another girl's name. Ever again. Isn't that crazy?"

It is, but I love it. I want Billie to be jealous over me. I want her snapping her teeth and staking out her territory. I'll never give her a reason to doubt me, but damn, it's fucking hot to see the angry flash in her green eyes.

"Insane." I unclip my own seat belt, ignoring her grumbles, and slide closer, pushing her thighs wide. I've barely skimmed my fingertips over the seam of her shorts when the engine cuts out.

We're home.

"Come on," I tell her, voice gruff, and push the car door open. "Pool house. Now."

Billie

"Why here?" I trip over the threshold to the pool house, the humid air kissing my cheeks. I can *feel* Eli prowling behind me, hot and strong and determined at my back, and it sends shivers skating down my spine.

He flicks a switch, lighting the pool up from inside and casting a gentle glow through the room.

"Unfinished business," he mutters, and tugs my jacket off my shoulders. He's pushy but patient, working the sleeve over my cast with infinite care. And once my jacket is tossed over a lounger, he pulls my top off next, his hungry gaze roving over my bare skin.

"Catch up." I bat at his shoulder, and he tugs his shirt off, grinning. He's sculpted and strong, covered in the kind of muscles that only come from real hard work out in the world and not from a gym. Pale scars cover his skin, and both fresh and old bruises.

I twist and show him the scrape on my lower back from surfing last week.

"Snap. This is from wiping out near the rocks."

He frowns, concerned, fingers ghosting over the marks, but he doesn't demand that I never surf again. No; he crowds closer, nibbling over my collarbone.

"Take me with you next time."

"Okay," I gasp. His mouth is scorching hot, his hands roaming over my bare skin, and the scrape of his teeth make me jump like I've been electrified. "If you take me climbing."

He chuckles, the sound vibrating across my throat.

"We'll have to get rid of these damn casts first."

I don't care. It's a future plan. With that, and the surfing, and Eli telling the driver, *take us home…*

Hope swells like a bubble in my chest.

This is really happening.

"Eli." He drops to his knees in front of me, working my button open and dragging my shorts down my legs. I kick off my sandals and step out of them, tugging at his shoulder. "Eli."

"Hmm?"

"The windows. People might see."

The pool house walls are basically glass, and with the light fading in the grounds, we must be lit up in here like a TV. Anyone could glance over from the gardens, or from a neighboring house, and see me standing here in my bra and panties with Eli on his knees.

Goosebumps ripple over my skin, and my breasts grow heavy and aching.

Huh. Guess I don't mind.

Eli nips at my hip bone, sucking a bruise onto the pale skin. He catches my eye and smirks as I unhook my bra and let it drop.

"Since when are models shy, baby?"

I bite my lip. My breasts are warm when I cup them, squeezing and pinching my nipples.

"You're right. We're not."

The knowledge that someone might see us makes my pussy throb. I widen my legs as Eli drags my panties down.

Maybe I *want* people to see us. To know that he's mine. To watch me ride his face, my head tipped back in pleasure.

So I don't hold back. When his fingers slide over my slick folds, brushing at my clit, I moan and buck my hips. I moan loud enough that it echoes around the pool house, and when Eli slings one of my legs over his shoulders, I rub myself on his tongue. He works me until I'm wound tight as a corkscrew, and only then does he push to his feet and unbutton his jeans.

"You gonna take my cock, baby?" His gaze is dark. Glittering. I nod, reaching for him with trembling hands. He laughs, the sound almost cruel, and god, I love that too. I follow him like a dazed puppy when he strides naked to the pool.

He doesn't get in. He sits on the side, legs dangling into the water. And when he pats his lap like I'm his little pet, I can't scramble fast enough onto his strong thighs.

"Fuck. Billie. I knew you'd be a needy little thing."

"Uh-huh." I grip his cock between us. I want to tease him, rub the head against my pussy until he's wound tight too, but he's done too good of a job. If I don't get him inside me, I'll explode.

I notch him at my entrance and sink down, wincing at the stretch. I get the first inch of him inside. The second. The third.

"Breathe, baby." He rubs his uninjured palm over my back, and I melt under his touch, sinking another inch lower. "Rock your pretty little hips."

I do as he says, rocking back and forth, and the slick slide of him in and out makes me whimper. Winding my arms around his neck, I press my face against Eli's throat and push down lower, lower, lower.

"You don't have to take it all, baby," he grits out.

I hiss out a breath. "Yes I do." But it's such a stretch, such a full feeling, and it's like he's *everywhere.* I'm glad my face is hidden. I bet my eyes are practically crossed.

The sudden crack of his palm against my ass makes me jerk, and heat floods my pussy. I moan and sink down easily, taking the final inch.

"I knew it." I can hear his grin above me. "I fucking knew you'd like that, sweet girl."

I'm not sweet, not really, and I set out to show him, rolling my hips and feeling every inch of his cock inside me. He's touching me everywhere, the ridges of him thick against my walls, and I moan as I roll my hips harder.

God. This is it. This is what all the fuss was about. My ass slams down against Eli's thighs as I bounce on his cock. I catch a glimpse of our reflections in the dark glass over his shoulder, and I look freaking *wild.* Flushed cheeks; hair falling out of my braid. Desperate and frantic, working myself on his lap. The sight makes my pussy clench and Eli moans, spanking my ass again, then grabs my hips and thrusts up into me.

I love it. Every bruising grip of his fingers, every crack of his palm against my ass. He's rough with me and treasures me all in the same go, and it makes me warm; loose-limbed and pliant. I tip my head back, gasping as he kisses down my throat before latching his hot mouth onto my nipple.

Something *tugs* in my pussy, a direct line from my breast, and I clamp down on his length, working my hips so fast they almost blur.

"Eli. *Eli.*"

"Do it. Come for me, baby."

I fall apart with a wrenching cry. I've never come like this before—like my insides are rearranging. Like my body is turning inside out. It goes on and on, my cry trailing off until I'm breathing through gritted teeth, and *still* I'm coming.

"Fuck!" Eli bites down on my shoulder, cock swelling even bigger, hot liquid spilling inside me. A huge ripple spreads through my core, seizing my muscles, then finally I slump in his arms, sticky and sated.

Our breaths are loud. Ragged. They bounce off the pool house walls. I shake my head against Eli's throat and he chuckles.

"I'm done. Dead. Bury me in the garden."

His hand strokes down my hair.

"If you think I'm ever letting you go again, you're out of your mind. You live here now, alright? You sleep in my bed. You eat my food. You take my cock. Billie Blue Walsh, you are *mine.*"

My arms wind tighter around his neck. Maybe it's crazy, but the thing is, I know it's my choice. Eli would never actually force me to do something I didn't want to do. And do I want to be his?

Hell yes. More than anything.

"I'm going to need a map," I mumble. "This house is freaking huge."

His laugh bounces off the walls. I burrow closer in his arms.

I'm his.

And he's mine.

Eli

Five years later

A summer breeze whistles through the mansion hallways. The doorways are propped open, pale window drapes fluttering in the wind, the scent of jasmine carried in from the gardens. Stilted piano scales echo in one room. Whoops of childish laughter sound in another.

My mansion is not cold or quiet anymore. My wife and I have been busy. Two twin brothers and a little girl's worth of busy.

I find Billie in the library, holding our one-year-old daughter up to gawp at the shelves. She waves a sticky, pudgy hand at the priceless leather spines, and I wince and muffle a laugh.

"You might be jumping the gun."

Billie grins at me over her shoulder. Her red hair is braided to the side again—one of my favorite sights since that first night all those years ago in the pool house. It's like a challenge, a red flag waved at a bull: *how wild can you make my hair this time?*

"Her father is a genius. Her older brothers are at the top of their classes too."

"Top in finger painting and spelling?"

"Yes." She sticks out her tongue, and the baby copies her. "So there."

"Must be twin magic." Billie hums as I step up to her back, dipping my head to kiss her neck. She tilts her head in welcome, and I lose myself in her scent. Green apple shampoo and sunshine.

A sticky hand lands on my cheek.

"Well, now." I scoop the baby out of her arms and bounce her against my chest. Baby Coral squeals, her pudgy arms waving. "Here's yet another female feeling jealous over me."

Billie snorts. "She can have you."

"Really?"

"Uh-huh."

I frown down at the baby. "That's not very nice, is it, Coral?"

"I'll show you nice," Billie breathes in my ear, her chest pressed against my back and her palm sliding over my stomach. She flicks my belt buckle. "Why don't you find the nanny? Then meet me in the gardens."

"Where?" I'm already striding to the doorway. My skin is flushed hot under my shirt, and I'm half hard in my jeans.

I never stop craving my wife. Not for a single day. Not for a goddamn hour. When she travels for fashion shoots, I go out of my mind. I always snap, flying to meet her after a couple of days.

Billie tuts. "If I tell you, that's cheating."

"And if you tease me, you'll be punished."

I turn in the doorway and level her a look. Billie smirks back, eyes dancing. She knows what she's doing. And I know what she wants.

How to give it to her.

How to make her scream.

By the time I'm done with her, the gardeners will be running for cover.

"Better get a head start. I won't go easy on you."

"I don't want you to!" she calls as she runs through the French doors. I curse under my breath, prowling through the mansion, searching for the world's best hidden nanny. I find her beside the piano, helping my giggling sons with their scales, and I kiss both boys on the forehead before leaving my children with her placid smile.

Billie. I need to find Billie.

It's a drumbeat. A pounding chorus in my blood. I plunge out of the nearest doors to the gardens and thunder down the stone steps.

My wife can run but she can't hide.

She's *mine*.

And I'm more than happy to remind her.

Get a free instalove story!

Want more sweet & steamy goodness?

Claim your copy of *Beauty & The Kingpin* when you sign up to my newsletter!

She's a florist. He's the king of the underworld.

The king of the underworld loves flowers. Not everyone knows that about him.

They know he rules the city with an iron fist; they know he suffers no fools and rarely shows mercy. But me—I know about his flowers.

I know other things, too. I know the shade of his blue eyes. The scent of his private office. The scrape of his teeth over my skin. But he doesn't know everything about me.

Like when I play, I play to win.

Claim your copy of Beauty & the Kingpin now!

Cassie Mint

About the Author

Cassie writes outrageous, OTT insta-love with tons of sugar and spice. She loves cookie dough, summer barbecues, and her gorgeous cat Missy.

You can connect with me on:

🌐 https://www.authorcassiemint.com

🔗 https://www.bookbub.com/authors/cassie-mint

🔗 https://www.amazon.com/~/e/B08VF8BPWG

Subscribe to my newsletter:

✉ https://www.authorcassiemint.com/newsletter